Also available from
Natalie Charles

Harlequin Romantic Suspense

The Seven-Day Target
The Burden of Desire
When No One Is Watching

Natalie Charles

The
Coffee
Girl

◆Cranberry Press◆

ISBN-13: 978-0-9862805-1-1

THE COFFEE GIRL

Cover design: Ebooklaunch.com
Copy Editor: Amanda Sumner

For Jess, my first partner in crime who teaches me everything I need to know about celebrity gossip. Love you!

THE COFFEE GIRL

CHAPTER ONE

SAM'S AFTER DARK was the only place in Archer Cove where you could get both a martini and an ice cream sundae, and I went there even though I didn't have money for either. I could sit on the rooftop deck and watch the sun set behind the cliffs. If Pete was tending bar, he'd give me a bowl of honey-roasted peanuts and a glass of water. Basically, he'd treat me like some kind of wild squirrel, if squirrels had laptops and occupied seats at the bar on Friday nights.

That night, I mounted the wooden stairs to the fourth floor, my laptop secured in my fashionably upcycled messenger bag. The June evening was still bright, but it would fade quickly. The white lights strung across the open roof were already lit, and the smells of Sam's Restaurant — marinara sauce and baked fish, garlic bread and spices — enveloped the space. I had a moment of panic when I saw Camille shaking a silver tumbler. We didn't know each other very well, and odds were good that she wouldn't take kindly to me perching on a stool and eating the free peanuts for a few hours. Then I saw Pete emerge from around the bar. "Hey, Wren!" He gave me a little wave and a smile.

"Pete." I bellied up and slumped into my favorite seat.

"Almost didn't recognize you." He gestured to his head. "What's with the hat?"

I reached up and brushed my fingers against the bill of my baseball cap. "Bad hair day."

More like the hot water in my apartment was spotty again, so I hadn't showered since getting off from work. I thought that stepping into a mist of "Hidden Garden" aerosol room freshener would help, but I still smelled like bacon and cinnamon toast, but now with a hint of toxic flowers. The baseball cap didn't help in the stink department, but it hid my batter-splattered hair. I wasn't in Sam's to pick up a date, and no one would smell me over the garlic bread.

Pete pointed at my laptop case. "You're the only one who comes in here to write. Don't most people pick cafés for that kind of thing?"

"You forget that I work in a bakery. It's not an escape from reality for me."

I was known as "the coffee girl" over at Hedda's, my family's bakery. Lattes, mochas, cappuccinos, straight-up cafe Americano — pick your pleasure. I wore an apron and kept a plastic cup marked "Tips!" in a hopeful scroll with blue marker. Every now and then, someone spared a nickel.

I'd become good at making foam. The first day after coming back from LA, I'd burned my fingers on the steam and splashed hot milk all over myself, but within a few days, I was steaming and frothing with something close to competence. Even my cousin Jessie noticed. Once she'd smiled at me as she set oversize cinnamon buns into the display case and said, "You're really getting the hang of it."

This is how little she expects from me, that she's impressed when I demonstrate aptitude with a machine advertised as being simple enough for a chimpanzee.

"What can I get you?" Camille approached with a guarded smile. She'd seen me before, and she knew I wasn't good for much in the way of tips. Maybe she was feeling hopeful.

"I've got it," Pete said. "Here, Camille, if you can take care of table three, that would be great."

As she sauntered off, Pete reached below the counter and set a bowl of peanuts next to me. "Thanks, buddy," I said, and grabbed a few.

"Enjoy those. We're changing over to popcorn."

"What? You're breaking my heart, Pete."

He wiped his hands on a black dishtowel. "Take it up with Sam. He's afraid of lawsuits, says there are too many peanut allergies."

"Damn." I liked my routine, and I was going to miss those peanuts. "I don't know how I feel about that."

"It's artisan popcorn, if that makes a difference." Pete again reached below the bar, this time producing a small silver bag. "Caramel and chocolate. You want to try a sample?"

"Of course."

While he poured the popcorn into a clean glass bowl, I pulled out my laptop. Pete slid the bowl next to me after helping himself to a few pieces of popcorn. "How's the writing going? Zombie vampires, right?"

"Zombie vampires in love," I said. "It's the new thing."

"Uh huh." He set a glass of ice water next to the bowls of popcorn and peanuts. "We get a mention when you're famous, right?"

"Are you kidding? You get a dedication."

The truth was, I wasn't writing a screenplay about zombie vampires, and the writing was not going well. I was on my fourth screenplay, a time travel story about a singer and the lovers over history who influenced her sultry style.

There in Sam's, where the night was falling around me and the bar was slowly becoming crowded with conversation, I was getting into a good rhythm when Pete set a martini glass in front of me. He may as well have thrown it in my face, I was so startled. "A cosmo," he explained. "From the gentleman by the rail."

I blinked a few times before it registered. Someone had just bought me a drink. I followed Pete's nod to the railing, where a dark-haired man stood looking out over the sea. He was wearing a dark-colored T-shirt that accentuated muscular arms, and he looked to be generally well constructed. I swallowed. "Him?"

Pete gave another nod. "Guy in the T-shirt standing over there. Said to give you whatever you were drinking, and I told him you were having water, so he said to give you a cosmo."

I brushed my hands down my jeans. In all the months I'd been coming to write at Sam's, this had never actually happened before. It wasn't that kind of a place, and I wasn't that kind of a person. "What should I do?"

Pete smiled. "Thank him? Tell him to piss off? Whatever you want." He turned to someone standing at the center of the bar. "What can I get you?"

This was a dilemma. If movies of the week and romance novels had taught me anything — and I liked to think they had — drinks with a strange man at a bar could lead to a myriad of possibilities. A night of passionate romance and an unexpected pregnancy, for example. I would fall pregnant and proudly assure him that no, I would raise this child on my own. Then, after a series of comic trials, we would fall in love. Or he could be the heir to an oil fortune, looking for a marriage of convenience in order to comply with the terms of his father's will. I would resist but would ultimately agree to the sham, and after a series of comic trials, we would fall in love. Or he could be a serial killer, in which case I would end up brutally murdered by the time the real story began.

I sighed. Odds were two out of three this wouldn't end with my head in a duffel bag, and maybe I'd get some material for my screenplay. I closed my laptop and slid it into my messenger, making sure to grab my cosmo as I made my way to the man by the railing. His back was to me, and now I could see that he was indeed very well built. I cleared my throat and tried to think of something clever to say. Maybe 'Don't jump?'

"How's your drink?"

Oh, he spoke first. That took the pressure off. "It's fine. Well, I haven't tried it yet, but it looks good." I held it up to the fading sunlight. "It's pink."

He half-turned his body, and that's when I saw he was very handsome, what with his dark coloring and angular jaw. Yes, I was confident he was either the heir to an oil fortune or a murderer. His cheeks were unshaven, and when he smiled, his teeth were white and straight. "I saw you sitting alone with your laptop. I thought you might like some company."

"Sure, why not. I just came here to work." I set my bag on the floor and leaned up against the rail, mirroring his pose.

"You work at the bar?"

"I write here. I like the noise."

"So you're a writer? Anything I'd know?"

Ah. I took a sip of my drink, and it burned my lips and tongue. This was where things usually got awkward, when I said that I wrote and people wanted to know whether I'd written anything important. Which I hadn't.

"Probably not," I said, and hoped he didn't care enough to ask more. He didn't.

"I'm Jax." He held out a hand.

"Wren."

"Red? That's your name? Like the color?"

"No, Wren. Like the bird." Curse my parents and their creative naming.

The corners of his mouth quirked upward. "You want to sit down? I promise I'm not trying to hit on you."

I hid my disappointment. Clearly this was not a marriage-of-convenience situation. Maybe he was going to stab me to death, after all. "I don't think that's a good idea. I came here to do some writing."

"Then take your cue from some of the greats. Your writing will go better after you get a couple of those in you," he said, nodding at the cosmo. "Come on. Sit down with me. I promise I won't bite."

I took another sip of the cosmo, feeling the warmth hit my veins. Liquid courage, my friends — it can make you do all kinds of crazy things. Like dance on tables or go home with a stranger—or, in this case, lose your head completely and agree to have drinks with a serial killer. "Okay," I said. "But it's your treat, and I'm ordering whatever I want. No strings attached."

He shrugged. "Sure. Whatever." He slid his fingers through his thick hair. "I wanted to talk to someone, that's all."

My feet were heavy as we trudged toward an empty table lit with a single tea light candle. He wanted to talk, and didn't that figure? People were always wanting to talk to me. My cousin Jessie said that I should have studied psychology instead of English. People loved to tell me all about their problems, and now it seemed I was about to have a cosmopolitan with one of the hottest men I'd ever met, and he was going to do nothing but use me as a sympathetic ear. The least he could do was take off his shirt and give me a good spanking afterward.

I climbed a little reluctantly into the high seat and took a larger sip of my drink. He was drinking something in an old-fashioned glass. A whiskey neat, maybe. Some manly drink. We were directly under the lights now, and although they were dim, I noticed a tattoo that wrapped around his upper arm. It was damn sexy.

My night was officially shot, my writing on the back burner. When Camille came to take our orders, I ordered an ice cream sundae with all the toppings. Jax sat back in his seat, more amused than disgusted. "Is that all? Are you sure you don't want a large pizza and wings to go with it?"

"I've got to save calories where I can." I set my drink aside and leaned forward, bracing myself. "So. You want to talk?"

Did he ever. He had arrived in town that morning. He claimed he was enjoying his time in Archer Cove, despite referring to the restaurants with adjectives like "serviceable." I sat and listened to him for what felt like forever. He didn't eat, but he liked his whiskey. He liked a lot of it.

During our conversation, I learned the following, which I've distilled for digestibility: Jax's mother was supportive of his career but thought he should settle down and have a family; his agent thought his image was damaged due to his "inability to commit" to one woman; he was young and wanted to have a good time, and why couldn't anyone see how misunderstood he was? I was mildly interested for half of my cosmo, then tuned out for the second half, then got through another fifteen minutes by focusing on my ice cream sundae, then wished I had the power of invisibility so I could make a quick escape.

At one point, I looked over at the bar and caught Pete's sympathetic gaze, but he didn't rescue me. We should have decided on some kind of a distress call, like a tug at my earlobe. Live and learn.

Jax took a breath and finished his drink. I leaned forward. "Am I allowed to speak?" I hadn't been able to get a word in edgewise in almost ten minutes.

He set his forearms on the table and leaned in. "You have beautiful eyes. I hope someone's told you that before."

I started. "Oh. Thank you." I toyed with the napkin in my lap. I'd been about to lecture him, and then he'd gone and thrown that compliment. Knocked me right off my game. "My dad has said that. They're just brown, though. Brown hair, brown eyes." Dullsville.

He smiled coolly. "They're not just brown. More like dark amber."

"I guess so."

I needed to return the compliment, and really, where to start? The guy was gorgeous. But I didn't want to seem like I was actually *into* him. It was all about choosing the right body part. "You have nice, uh —" Hair? Hands? Lips? "— teeth. Very straight and, you know, white."

Nice teeth? I wanted to spontaneously combust.

Jax laughed. "Thank you. And hey, I'm sorry if I talked your ear off. I sometimes ramble when I have a lot on my mind."

"You're using me as therapy, which is fine. Lots of people do, and I'm used to it. And I understand that women fling themselves at you and that you find it impossible to commit to one. I mean, I guess I don't understand that at all, but I'll take your word for it that it's been a problem."

I paused when I noticed his eyes could barely focus on me and he looked as if he might fall asleep at the table at any moment. I could keep going, knowing he wouldn't digest a word, or I could thank him for the drinks and call him a cab. Jax was looking less like a serial killer and more like a guy who'd had life too easy.

He turned his glass in the candlelight. "Please, continue."

I studied him, and then realization congealed slowly in my brain. "Wait, you're an actor, aren't you? Jax Cosgrove." Of course. Half of Hollywood was in town for the film festival.

"You're just realizing it now?" He smiled sadly. "You have no idea what that does to my ego."

"Sorry, I've been avoiding Hollywood for a few months." I dragged my spoon through the remnants of my sundae. "Griff Dannel is my ex-boyfriend."

"Really?" He raised his eyebrows. "From when, high school?"

"Try six months ago." I couldn't keep the bitterness from creeping into my voice.

He took a renewed interest, studying me over the flickering candle. "Are you an actress?"

"No. I mean, not really. I've done some small roles here and there. It's how Griff and I met."

A cool breeze passed and sent goosebumps across my arms. My acting career was like bad sex: awkward, forgettable, and over quickly. I'd taken a few small parts to learn the business, but I was much more comfortable behind the scenes, writing screenplays. Alone with my computer, holed up in a room like a common misanthrope. It just felt so much safer that way.

"Griff's with Poppy Hayes now."

"Yeah, and I'm pretty sure there was some relationship overlap, if you know what I mean."

Things with Griff had ended in a colossally horrible fashion that was *not at all* my fault. If someone were to construct a big-screen metaphor of our breakup, it would involve some kind of car explosion and an action heroine fleeing the scene in a white tank spotted with grime, her hair flying. I would be the action heroine, obviously. Griff would be the terrorist who blew up the car. I took a sip of my water. "I don't actually want to talk about it."

19

"Sounds like drama. I hadn't pegged you as the type, because of that hideous hat." He raised his glass again, and then tried to drain any liquid at the bottom. "My career as a leading man is as good as over before it began, anyway."

"Why, because you're a womanizer?"

His mouth rose in a half-smile. "I'm unfairly portrayed by the media, Wren. And it doesn't help that I keep getting cast in womanizer roles. My publicist says it's a case of art imitating life, or vice versa."

"So start telling people you're a method actor."

He ignored me and pushed his glass aside. "She left me a voice mail message this morning."

"Who?"

"My publicist. Let's just say that it wasn't kind. She thinks I'm going to be left to supporting actor roles unless I walk the straight and narrow. Who wants to settle for straight and narrow, anyway?"

"Uh, no one," I said quickly. "How boring. Anyway, I'm really sorry, Jax. What a stupid business Hollywood is."

He closed his eyes, but didn't answer. For a second I thought he was going to burst into tears, and I was bracing myself. Then he slumped forward and began to slide off his seat. I rushed to his side. "Jeez. You okay?" He was heavy.

From out of nowhere, Pete appeared and helped me to lower him to the ground. "Guy can't hold his liquor."

Jax was sitting up, but he was shaky. His arms hung limply at his side as he grumbled, "I'm tired."

"You're something, all right," Pete said. "Where are you going? We'll call a cab."

Cabs in Archer Cove basically didn't exist. We'd have to call a dispatcher two towns over and wait for someone to come. It could be a long time, and since I was feeling responsible for Jax's well-being, I was selfishly relieved when he mumbled, "The inn."

"I can walk him back," I said to Pete, hoping that Jax could meet me halfway by standing up. "It's only two blocks."

Pete wasn't convinced. "You sure? How much have you had?"

"Just the cosmo, and that was almost two hours ago. I'm not even driving."

"But you don't know this guy. I don't want him taking advantage of you."

I was touched by Pete's concern, but confident I would be fine. "I'll just get him to his room and leave."

Pete seemed satisfied with that answer. "If you get into any trouble —"

I nodded, and we both helped Jax to his feet. He swung this way and that, but otherwise mustered the presence of mind to walk out of the bar and down the stairs. "Tell him to come back tomorrow to settle the tab." Even Pete must have known that getting Jax to return to pay was kind of a tall order.

We hit the sidewalk, me and my new buddy Jax. I had him propped up against my shoulder. He kept muttering, "I'm fine, I'm fine," into my hair.

"You're not fine. You're blasted," I said. "You're going to be feeling this in the morning."

"I'm just tired," he groaned, his alcohol-soaked breath hot on my ear. "You're...a nice girl," he crooned. Then he reached for my breast, and I jabbed a sharp elbow into his ribs.

We continued the walk down Elm Grove, hobbling past restaurant row, which boasted the best dining in Archer Cove and was still crowded even at this late hour. Fortunately, Jax looked so inebriated that pedestrians gave us a wide berth, and we were able to move relatively swiftly down to Bishop's Place. I could have wept with relief to see Archer Cove Inn rising in the distance. *Almost there.*

The inn was quite large, with approximately forty guest rooms and several guest cottages. Having grown up in Archer Cove, I'd never actually stayed there myself, but I'd always admired the sweeping porch that wrapped around the front and sides and overlooked the ocean. Now that same porch was occupied with guests and visitors enjoying evening cocktails and light jazz, and Jax and I were quickly becoming a distracting spectacle.

We climbed the wide front steps that led to the gracious entry, where an enormous crystal vase filled with roses — pink, white, and yellow — occupied our line of vision. Mine, at least. I'm not sure Jax was able to focus on anything.

"Oh for the love of —" Anna Tumblesby, the owner of the inn, came flying from behind the front desk. "What on earth…?"

"Hi, Anna. It's me. Wren."

"Oh heavens." She set one hand over her heart. "Honey, I didn't recognize you. Nice hat."

"Uh, thanks. This is Jax. He says he's a guest at the inn."

Until that moment, it hadn't occurred to me that he might be mistaken, given his state, and then what would I do? But fortunately Anna nodded and whispered, "He's a VIP. He's in the executive suite."

"Mind if I take him there? He needs to lie down."

"I'll say." Anna was a vision of white, from her white linen jacket and matching pants to her light blonde hair. She was full-figured and soft in both appearance and manners, but that didn't stop her from assisting me by reaching across Jax's lower back and saying, "Come on. It's on the third floor, and our elevator is out until tomorrow."

Together, one step at a time, we reached the executive suite. As I stepped inside, my breath was stolen by the bay window that captured a panoramic view of the Atlantic and the mansions on the cliffs, lit against the darkness. The entryway was marble, the woodwork appeared hand-carved and ornate. The decor was rounded out by crystal lamps and silk linens.

We helped Jax to the bed, sitting him down and then flinging his legs on top of the mattress. Anna set her hands on her hips, every bit the image of the disappointed mother. "Mr. Cosgrove," she said, clucking her tongue. "Are you going to be okay, sir?"

"Just tired. I...took a pill."

"You did what, now?" I went from irritated to concerned. "What kind of a pill?"

"Valium. This morning. For the plane." He flung one arm across his eyes and reached for me with the other one. "Stay here. Please?"

I looked at Anna, who simply returned my gaze helplessly. "I don't...don't you have anyone else you're traveling with? Can't they stay with you?" *Can't* anyone else *stay with you?*

"He came in alone," Anna said. "Told me his agent isn't coming in for a few more days."

"Please?" he whispered. "What if I die?"

I gave a long glance at Anna, who just shook her head. "Fine. I'll stay here for a little while. But I swear, if you touch me, I'll cut you."

I didn't have anything to cut him with, but Jax didn't seem capable of doing much of anything but whining and passing out. "Okay," he murmured as he rolled onto his side. "Deal."

Anna pursed her lips, clearly disapproving of her guest's unbecoming state. "Mr. Cosgrove, you let me know if there's anything else you need tonight. Just hit that little red button on the phone. You too," she said to me, lowering her voice.

I nodded. "I'm only going to be here for a little while, until I'm sure he's okay."

Anna nodded. "You owe her one, Mr. Cosgrove. You hear me?" Then with a little wave to me, she turned and left the room.

I slumped onto a leather couch that was surprisingly soft and inviting. Jax didn't move, other than to mumble something every now and then. I waited for a bit, thinking I should make my way home. I was only four, maybe five blocks from my apartment. I don't know why I didn't just get up and leave. I kept thinking about Jax saying that he took a Valium, and I thought it made sense to have someone there, just in case he stopped breathing. I wouldn't be able to live with myself if I left and he died.

I removed my hat and set it on a table, then shook out my hair. The couch was soft, and my body ached because I'd been up early, and the pillows were perfectly stuffed and velvet...

He woke first and shook my shoulder. "Hey," he said. Then more insistently, "Hey."

"Oh." I sat upright, rubbed my eyes, and glanced at the blue numbers on the digital alarm clock. "Shit." Five o'clock. That meant I had half an hour to get to work.

I slipped into my shoes, grabbed my bag, and headed for the door. "Wait!" Jax said behind me. "You don't have to —"

"Thanks for the ice cream!"

I pulled on my hat, opened the door, and stepped into the hall. Stopping at home was out of the question, but if I ran to work, I might have time to wash my face in the bathroom sink, and maybe Jessie would have an extra toothbrush. Just...shit.

I broke into a run when I hit the front porch, feet flying across the boards. All I could think about was reaching work in time to avoid my dad's suspicious gaze. I never even saw the woman taking my picture.

I was out of breath by the time I made it to Jessie's apartment and knocked on the robin's-egg blue door. She was fully dressed, but she had a towel on her head and a toothbrush in her mouth. "Wren? What's going on?"

"Long story. Can I use your shower?"

She stepped aside, staring at me as I entered. She removed her toothbrush. "Is everything okay?"

"It's fine." I set my laptop on the kitchen table and removed my hat. I felt grimy, there was no other word for it. "Do you think I could borrow some clothes, too?"

Jessie left the room without a word and returned moments later with a pile of clean clothes and a towel. "Did you pull an all-nighter or something?"

"I spent the night out." When Jessie's eyebrows hit the ceiling, I hastily added, "It's not what you think. Trust me."

"Too bad." She resumed brushing her teeth, and this time, she spoke to me around the toothbrush. "I have more soap in the cabinet."

I showered quickly and dressed in the simple black T-shirt and jeans Jessie had provided. The underwear was more complicated. I settled on turning yesterday's pair inside out.

The hot water went some way toward clearing my head, but I must have still looked terrible because the first thing Jessie asked me when I stepped out of the bathroom was "Are you okay to work?"

"I have to be okay to work." Not because of any valiant work ethic, but because I was broke, and I needed the paycheck. I finger combed my hair. It was the best I could do under the circumstances. It all was.

Jessie went around the apartment, straightening the pillows on the couch and opening the white curtains that hung over the picture window. "You probably haven't eaten. I'll make you breakfast when we get down there. I've been working on my caramel truffle recipe."

"Chocolate for breakfast sounds good."

"Oh, sorry. Those were two different thoughts. But if you want a truffle for breakfast, that's fine."

Jessie lived in the three-bedroom apartment above the bakery, which sounds more spacious than it is. Lately, it seemed to be shrinking as she compiled the tools of her after-hours chocolate-making hobby: a copper kettle, various mixers, candy molds, and a marble slab. After leaving Hedda's, she would come home and develop her own caramel and ganache recipes. In the time I'd stayed with her before finding my apartment, I'd probably gained ten pounds.

I darted a glance around the room as Jessie grabbed her keys. "Where's Prince Travis?"

"Oh, I stuck him behind the door," she said nonchalantly. "I had some friends over a couple nights ago."

Prince Travis was a family heirloom: our great Aunt Esther's beloved pet silver fox, who'd been preserved for all eternity after his death by a taxidermist who mistakenly believed Esther would invite him to bed for the favor. After Aunt Esther passed away, we all wondered who'd be the lucky heir. Turns out it was Jessie. "They asked me to move him," she explained. "It's like it bothered them to have cocktails while staring at a taxidermic fox. Weird. You still have to pat his head on the way out. For luck."

I reached down and dutifully patted his stiff black head. "*Stay*, Travis."

Jessie locked up and we headed down the rickety gray back steps to Hedda's Bakery, where my dad already had the ovens in full swing. The air was filled with the scents of powdered sugar mixed with cinnamon, warm bread, and coffee. These were the smells of my childhood. If I closed my eyes, I was ten years old again.

"Good morning, ladies." My dad was whistling to himself as he baked, wearing a white T-shirt, khaki shorts, and an apron. "Another busy day."

"Busy is good." Jessie grabbed an apron from the hook. "What can I get you for breakfast, Wren?"

"You didn't eat this morning?" Dad sliced some dough for cinnamon rolls and set them in a baking pan.

"Uh, no. Just…" I glanced at Jessie. "Overslept."

Dad resumed whistling, and I released my breath. It was never a good idea to pique Dad's interest.

"How about an egg sandwich?" Jessie offered.

"Sounds good." I lifted a forlornly utilitarian light-blue apron and walked into the cafe.

It's pretty much my personal hell to work in a bakery, even if it belongs to my family. My cooking acumen stops at boiling water for noodles, though I've been known to microwave a mean leftover here or there, or build a decent sandwich. Still, I can't bake, which is why I ended up on the coffee maker.

I fired up the machine and made myself a latte, figuring I should get caffeinated before we opened. At least I got breakfast sandwiches. Jessie served up two hand-sliced pieces of rye toast stuffed with two eggs over medium, two slices of tomato, thinly sliced red onion, avocado spread, and melted cheddar cheese. It was messy and absolutely perfect. "Who's better than you, Jessie?" I managed through a mouthful.

"I'll add that to your tab," she said, and swatted at my behind with a rolled-up towel.

CHAPTER TWO

YOU KNEW JUST by looking at him that Griffin Dannel was going to be a star. He had that charisma and the good looks to go along with it. We met on a small indie film, and he invited me out for dinner. That was it. Presto! Our love was as instant as dehydrated soup. We moved in together because we wanted to, but also because it made sense. I was a struggling writer, he was a struggling actor, and rent was pricey. We ate macaroni and cheese and drank tap water and we were happy. Then Griff hit. Big time.

He was cast in a summer blockbuster — in the leading role, no less. He was a hot new face on a hot new franchise that involved sex, spies, and explosions. Suddenly people stopped us on the street for autographs. The paparazzi followed us. I suppose it was naive of me to think Griff and I would weather his fame. One celebrity blogger ran an entire post about how it was "sweet" that Griff was still standing by his "average" girlfriend despite his celebrity. "He could have any woman in the world," she'd written. "For now, he seems content to settle."

"That's bullshit, Wren," Griff had said when he'd found me curled up on the couch in the fetal position. He was wearing a T-shirt with the sleeves cut off, and his collar was ringed with sweat after another one of his sessions with his personal trainer. He lifted the front of the shirt and swept his face. "You can't pay any attention to that crap."

I wanted to believe him. You want to believe that the person you love to the stars and back loves you the same distance. But I think those bloggers hit home. I knew that as much as I adored Griff, he was settling for me.

I didn't find out about Poppy until the neighbor went on vacation and asked me to feed her cats. They were out of food, and I'd gone to the convenience store to buy more. So there I was, emptying a basket of Fancy Feline onto the checkout counter, when I saw the new edition of *Star Sightings*. On the cover was an image of Griffin holding hands with reality television star Poppy Hayes and the headline, "It's Official!"

"Would you like to buy a lottery ticket, miss?"

I was jarred from my intestine-wringing dismay by the checkout clerk's question. "Sorry?"

"Anything else tonight?"

I calmly reached beside me and lifted a copy of the magazine. "Just this. Please."

When I got home, I left it in the brown paper bag and hid it under the mattress. I fed the cats, made some tea, and stared at the wall for a bit. When Griff came home, I didn't say anything. In fact, I didn't even mention it until two days later, and only then because I'd come home to find Griff's suitcase open on the bed. "You're finally leaving?" I said.

"Yeah." He didn't make eye contact.

I thought about retrieving my magazine, maybe brandishing it at him with a string of expletives and vitriol. But I didn't. I didn't want to confront those photos. A small part of me even hoped he might change his mind.

"You've made a fool out of me." My voice cracked.

He didn't say anything else as he tossed his clothes into the suitcase. Neither did I. Two years together, and then he was gone.

"Put that in your pipe and smoke it," had been my mother's response. I'd called her when I found out about Griff.

"Mom, what does that even *mean*? What am I supposed to be smoking here?"

I was sitting on my couch, wondering what had possessed me to seek out my mother about boy troubles when I was twenty-eight years old. It wasn't the idea of seeking out my mother. It was the idea of seeking out *my* mother.

"Poppy Hayes," she said. "Put Poppy Hayes in your pipe and smoke her."

I'm sure I blinked a few times. "I still don't see —"

"It is what it is, Wren. That's what the expression means." I imagined her waving one hand as if swatting at flies and then taking a sip of zinfandel. "So Griffin has moved on to someone new. There are plenty of other fish in the sea. You've looked around, right? You keep your eyes open when you walk down the street? You live in the land of beautiful people. You'll find someone new."

Words of wisdom from my mother, who flubs clichés and thinks people are as interchangeable as goldfish. Jessie was more concerned for my well-being. She advised me to stay off the Internet. "Those bloggers are bottom-feeders. Nothing but lies and rumors."

"Is that right?" I replied. "I wouldn't know. I don't read those blogs."

This was a lie. I devoured those blogs, usually with a pint of ice cream. Griff and Poppy were heading out to the beach — check out her killer abs! Poppy was recently spotted wearing a canary diamond on her left ring finger — are wedding bells in the air? Once I'd read about them grabbing frozen yogurt at a spot in Malibu, and I'd actually shouted at my computer screen, "You're lactose intolerant, you jackass!" It was as if the breakup had fostered some kind of pathology.

Because when it came down to it, I had loved him. I had loved Griff Dannel, and he broke my heart by cheating on me with Poppy Hayes. The experience had rubbed a part of me raw, and each time I thought I was healed, the wound would open again.

I was preparing a mocha latte when I heard Jessie curse under her breath and say, "Don't look now, Wren."

Of course I looked, as I do any time someone tells me not to. At first, I only saw the crowd across the street, the paparazzi and the autograph seekers. Then a tall, lanky blonde pulled away from the group, shaking her head and holding up one hand. No more, she was saying. I could read her lips from there. No more. And she reached behind her to grab her companion's hand. The hand I used to hold.

"Griff and Poppy." The names tumbled out of my mouth. "Dammit."

I watched them like a voyeur observing a car wreck. They were a gorgeous couple, suntanned and fit. She was wearing aviator sunglasses and a pink shirtdress that exposed a mile of bronze leg. He was more casual in jeans that were strategically torn and a dark T-shirt that fit his muscular frame like a glove. His hair was longer now. He wore it tousled, and he'd had it highlighted.

We used to make fun of people who looked like he looked now, men who bought jeans pre-ripped and added foil highlights to their hair. I used to know who he was. I observed the shift with more curiosity than sadness. Then I realized they were coming across the street. To Hedda's. Where I was.

I glanced down at my plain black T-shirt, denim jeans, and flat, rubber-soled sneakers. The uniform of the damned. "I have to go," I said to Jessie.

"Are you kidding? Look at this line!" she hissed. Then she shook her head. "No, you're right. Just finish whatever you're doing. I'll handle it."

I swore under my breath and fumbled the coffee filter in my hands, all the while hoping to God I could foam that mocha latte and slink away to the back before they could see me. I was wearing no makeup and my hair was pulled back into a messy bun and secured with a piece of twine I'd found in the kitchen. I was wearing clothes I'd borrowed from Jessie and yesterday's underwear, inside out. I kept my eyes on my work, the ostrich strategy. *If I don't see you, then you don't exist...*

"Hello, Wren."

He'd come right up to my side of the counter, bypassing the line that wound around the interior of the bakery. His voice was smooth and cool, his gaze set to level with mine, and when I looked him in the eye, I detected a hint of amusement that made me wish I could spontaneously combust.

I pulled myself together enough to say, "Griff. What a surprise."

"I heard you'd come back here," he said. He stuffed his hands in his pockets as he looked around, rocking back on his heels. "Nice place."

I followed his gaze, trying to get a sense of his appraisal. The white walls needed painting, and the old

35

advertisements on the wall for flour and eggs might be regarded by some as kitschy. We'd had the display cases for as long as I could remember, and the white and black tiles on the floor had seen better days. People came here because my dad was the best baker around, not because the decor was top-notch. "I've always liked it," I said.

"So you're gone from LA? For good?"

"Yeah." I shrugged like it was no big thing. "I figured it was time to take a break from it all. You know, the grind." I set the mocha latte on the table beside me and said, "Carl!" And then I saw a flash of pity in Griff's eyes, and I wanted to die. "I love it here," I added, wiping my hands on my apron. "You know that."

"You're not writing anymore?"

"Oh no, I'm still writing. I'm working on a new screenplay. It's generated some interest."

That last part was true, because Jessie wanted to read it when I was done. The silence between us stretched, so I cleared my throat and said, "You must be in town for the film festival."

"Yeah. *A Night in Venice* is playing. You remember, I got that role right when —" He scratched the side of his nose. "Back around, when..."

"I understand." I knocked some coffee grounds against the trash a bit too violently and sent some clumps flying to the floor.

Poppy was off studying the pies in one of the side displays, but she strutted over then, her nose in the air. "I thought we were getting a coffee," she said. Snarled, really. She kept her profile to me.

"We are," Griff answered. "I thought we'd stop here."

Clearly, Griff had failed to run the reunion by Poppy. She leveled a glare at him that I could see even through those sunglasses. "No, I thought we were going to a coffee place."

"This *is* a coffee place," he said.

To my left, Jessie was counting out change from the register. "To translate to Neanderthal, I think she finds it strange that you're in here talking to your ex-girlfriend," she said. "Frankly, she has a point."

"Who asked you?" Poppy snapped. She lifted her Ferragamo bag higher on her shoulder. "This town is such a dump."

Jessie slammed the register drawer shut. "Sorry, are we not living up to your standards, princess? At least people around here know better than to go trolling for men in other people's bedrooms."

It was at about this point that I began praying for something to knock me unconscious until they were gone and Jessie had calmed down. I rubbed at my temples. "So, can I get you anything?"

Griff's eyes widened with confusion. "No. I just wanted to say hi."

"Do you see that line behind you?" I waited while he turned. "Those are all paying customers who have things to do today, and I don't want to be the one who delays them."

When he continued blinking, Jessie leaned over and added, "That means the interview is over, buddy. She's moved on."

A cloud passed over Griff's face, but he didn't respond except to say, "Fine. Have a nice life, Wren."

He grabbed Poppy's hand and they left. When they reached the sidewalk, he made a show of kissing her right in front of the window. I bit my lip. It hurt.

"What a snake," Jessie snarled. "Can you believe the nerve of that guy?"

Dad called from the kitchen. "Wren? Phone call."

Jessie and I exchanged a glance. "Who would call me?"

She looked at the line. "Might as well go. Please hurry back."

"Of course."

I was still shaking when I reached the phone. "Hello?"

"Hello, gorgeous," crooned a male voice.

I'd had just about enough of games for one day. "Who the hell is this?"

"Hey, easy now. It's Jax."

"What the —? How did you get this number?"

"It's on the Internet. And so is our love affair."

I groaned. "I have no idea what you're talking about, and I have better things to do."

"Meet me for lunch."

"I can't. I'm working."

"Then come by later, I don't care. Whenever. I'll be here."

"What's this about, Jax?"

"I want to thank you for last night. And I want to apologize."

"Apology accepted. Don't worry about it."

"Wren." His voice was insistent. "Please. Stop by the inn later. There's something I need to tell you."

I slumped my shoulder against the wall, all the while thinking about Jessie alone behind the counter. I could have argued, but what was the harm in stopping by to see Jax, anyway? And really, did I think I had something better to do?

"Okay," I said. "I'll stop by at some point this afternoon. I'll give you a call before I leave."

"Good. And Wren? Be sure to wear the hat."

He hung up before I had the chance to respond.

It was nearly three o'clock before I arrived at Archer Cove Inn. The previous night's lousy sleep and the humiliation at the bakery were weighing on my muscles, but I felt better after a hot shower. I'd put on what I felt to be a presentable blue sundress. When I arrived at the inn, I went in without saying hello to anyone and proceeded directly up the stairs to the VIP suite. I only had to knock twice before Jax opened the door. He grinned when he saw me, striking one muscular arm against the doorjamb. "Well well well," he said, running his gaze across my figure. "Look at you."

"Don't be gross." I swept underneath his arm. "So? I'm here. And I wore the damn hat."

"Good." He drew a circle in the air with his finger in my direction. "Interesting dress. The casual look."

"I like this dress." I tried not to sound injured.

"Of course. I sometimes forget that not everyone enjoys couture."

He closed the door behind us and locked it, and for a second I thought that maybe I should have mentioned to someone that I would be seeing Jax. Maybe he was going to kill me now. "Jax —"

"I ordered you lunch." He gestured to a silver tray on which sat two silver platters. Beside it, champagne was chilling in a silver bucket. "Let's go out to the balcony."

I followed his gesturing arm to a set of French doors that opened wide to the outside. A small table for two waited for us, covered by a linen tablecloth and set with silver, china and crystal. A vase in the center held a single red rose. It was altogether too romantic.

I turned to him. "Look, I think there's been a misunderstanding —"

He reached up to stroke my cheek. "There's no misunderstanding. Let's have lunch." Sensing my hesitation, he sighed and said, "Come on. When was the last time you ate filet mignon and lobster tail with a movie star on a balcony overlooking the ocean?"

He continued past me, not waiting for my response. Assuming the sale. I doubted anyone told a man like Jax no. The woman in me had her dignity hanging by a thread. The writer in me wanted to see what he was up to. The writer won.

Jax was gentleman enough to pull out my chair, and he even gave me the better seat so that I had a full view of the water. He then set about uncovering our lunches, setting out a fragrant meal of filet mignon, lobster, and rosemary-seasoned fingerling potatoes. Then he presented a bowl filled to the brim with bread rolls, still warm from the oven. He was grinning again as he sat across from me and set the linen napkin in his lap. Beaming, really. I should have been suspicious, but I was also half-starved and began devouring my meal.

"See? Just two people having lunch and pleasant conversation. Oh!" He snapped his fingers. "The champagne."

He pushed back his chair and swept through the French doors. A moment later, I heard the pop of the cork and he came back to the balcony. "For you, madame." He filled my flute generously.

"Thank you."

He helped himself to some champagne before resuming his seat. Then he lifted his glass. "To us."

I set my fork and knife down on the plate. "All right. What gives, Jax? What's this all about?"

That grin again. I'd thought it was happiness, but now I realized it was the cat that swallowed the canary. My stomach clenched. Was he making a fool out of me?

"You haven't seen, I presume?"

"Seen? Seen what?"

Instead of answering, he reached into his pocket and retrieved a cell phone. He focused on the screen, typed something, and then handed it to me. "Celebrity Burn, baby doll. You and I are setting the blogosphere on fire."

I squinted at the screen, then enlarged it. No. The photo — oh, good lord. It was a picture of me leaving the hotel that morning, my head down, my hair covered by my hat. The caption read: "Walk of Shame."

"Oh God." My fingers flew to cover my mouth. "Oh my good God."

"That's what you said last night, too." He gave me a wink and a grin.

"What are you, ten years old?" I showed him the screen. "What does this mean?"

He sat back in his seat and took a sip of champagne. "Read it, love."

But before I could snap, "Don't call me 'love,'" I saw it for myself:

Looks like love is in the air at the Archer Cove Film Festival. Hollywood bad boy Jax Cosgrove was spotted at a local inn with a mysterious beauty. They entered together, and she left his room early this morning — apparently believing that the paparazzi would still be sleeping. But we caught her! Of course, knowing Jax, tomorrow morning will bring yet another lucky lady who gets to do the walk of shame across his bedroom.

I tilted my head. "Wow. Are you *sure* you're the one who leaves first after a one-night stand? Anyway, what does this have to do with that blog?"

He pulled his chair closer to mine and took a conspiratorial tone. "My agent calls this morning. She's pulling out her hair over this. She took me to lunch last week and lectured me on the importance of...*behaving* myself. No more parties. No more one-nighters. I'm supposed to be a respectable bachelor. Then this news breaks. Suddenly I'm sleeping with some mysterious beauty in Archer Cove."

"Okay. Then we'll come out and explain what really happened."

"No one wants to read about how I didn't sleep with you, Wren. They want the gossip."

I frowned. "Jax, let's pretend I'm dense. You have to explain it —"

He looked straight into my eyes. "I want you to pretend to date me."

"What?" My tongue stopped cooperating and I began to stammer. "I can't — I don't even — what the —"

"It's simple. Accompany me to a few things while I'm here. Be the mysterious beauty in my life for a bit. Smile for the camera. Pretend you like me. Maybe I'll fly you out to LA in a few weeks, parade you around town."

"*Parade* me around —"

"It's perfect," he continued, easing back into his chair. "I don't want a relationship. Not really. I just want the part of Ben. You apparently can't stand me, so there's no reason you'd develop feelings, and you're some small-town girl. Not at all my type, so..." He beamed. "Perfect."

I crumpled my linen napkin in my fist and threw it at my plate. "This isn't right. I'm not going to sit here while you insult me." I stood to leave.

"Oh, come on." He rose and placed himself in front of the French door, grasping my wrist gently between his fingers. "We're practically old friends. I thought you knew when I was teasing."

"We are *not* old friends. You only bought me a drink because you thought I was some dummy girl who'd be tickled to be hit on by an actor. Unfortunately for you, I have my pride."

Pride that was in tatters at that point. Jax had asked me to meet him so he could essentially proposition me, and there I was, wearing a sundress and a damn hat and drinking his champagne like some...*groupie*. "I have things going on," I said. "Big things."

Even as I made the statement, I recognized it for what it was. What did I have going on, exactly? A gig foaming milk at my family's bakery? A box filled with screenplays that no one would ever read? An award-winning screenplay in my mind? My one-bedroom apartment looked out into the back of a restaurant called Crabby Andy's. My clothes smelled like fried clam strips and I could *still* barely afford the rent. What was I so pleased about in my life?

I forced myself to look him directly in his dark eyes, to stare him down with my convictions so that he could see how wrong he was. *I have stuff to do.* But he wasn't sneering at me. His eyes were almost kind, almost pleading, and it was *almost* enough to make me agree to help him.

"I know you have a life," he said. "I know this is a lot to ask. I'm willing to make it worth your while."

I froze. "Worth my while? What does that mean, exactly?"

"I'll pay you."

I laughed. "No way. I'm pretty sure that would make me a prostitute." Didn't need to check that one off my bucket list.

He was dead serious. "Name your price."

I reached up to tuck my hair behind my ears, rattled by his composure. Instead of my hair, I found my baseball cap. I dropped my hands to my side. "I can't date you for money."

"Twenty thousand dollars? Fifty?"

My mind went blank. Fifty thousand dollars would cover a lot of rent payments. Still. "It's not going to happen, Jax."

He frowned as he studied a spot on the floor, looking so upset that I felt that pang of sympathy again. It was flattering to be desired, even if it was for a fake romance. Besides, I'd read a novel or two where this exact scenario even turned into true love. Still, it wouldn't happen here.

I tentatively put a hand on his shoulder. "I'm sure you'll get that role. You *are* perfect for Ben."

He looked up again with that striking intensity. No wonder women went weak-kneed around him. "How about this: I'll help you sell that screenplay."

My heart skipped. "Wh-what screenplay?" None of the many I'd written were any good.

"Hodges Brennan is producing *The Rose Garden*. If I get that part, I'll give him your screenplay."

I withdrew my hand, which was beginning to tremble. My work wasn't up to par, I was certain. Not up to Hodges Brennan's standards, for sure. I couldn't exactly admit that to Jax, though. "He wouldn't — you can't make him buy my screenplay."

"No, but I can hand deliver it to him. And if he doesn't want it, I'll hand deliver it to someone who does." He stepped closer, closing the space between us to inches rather than feet. "What do you say?"

My head had started to buzz with the possibilities. When I'd been dating Griff, he'd been a struggling actor and I'd been a struggling writer. He'd only recently had his big break, and it wasn't like I could call him up and ask him to help me out. But the only way anyone accomplished anything in Hollywood was to know someone who knew someone. Up to that point, I'd never known anyone.

I had a choice: I could accept that one of my dreams would never come true, or I could take a chance on Jax.

I swallowed. "Okay. I'll pretend date you, and you'll promise to try to sell my screenplay. But on one condition: you can't date *me*. I can't have paparazzi knocking me over and crowding the bakery. Keep my name out of it."

Practical, I thought. I'd also considered that dating Jax publicly might lead Griff to believe I was trying to make him jealous. I couldn't give him that satisfaction.

Jax wasn't buying it. He narrowed his gaze. "This sounds high maintenance."

"So?"

"So, you're in a polyester-blend sundress, Wren," he said, darting his fingers beneath the strap of my dress. The contact sent a shiver bolting across my skin. "You're medium maintenance on your best day. Don't you want to impress your girlfriends? How many of them have slept with box-office gold?" He grinned as he tightened his grip around my strap.

"You don't know my friends. If they found out I'd slept with you, they'd probably take me for counseling. Vain actor who believes he's a gift to womankind? No thanks, buddy. I've been down that path before." I brushed his fingers away with a dry laugh. "This is one of my conditions. Take it or leave it."

"Fine, whatever. Be someone else." Jax looked down. "What, we need to shake on this?" He grasped my outstretched hand and gave it a few pumps. "There. Consider it signed in blood."

I reached over to the table and lifted my flute of champagne. The view from this spot really was lovely. Much nicer than the view of the Dumpster behind Crabby Andy's. I finished my drink in one gulp.

Jax took a seat and tilted his chair back on two legs. "Can you stay for a while? You should plan to be here for a couple of hours at least. For verisimilitude. There's a party I'd like you to attend on Friday night, too. It's over at a mansion on the cliffs. Great Barrington, if I remember correctly."

"Sure, I can stay. Keep the champagne coming." I pulled out my chair and propped my feet up on the railing, delighting in the way Jax raised his eyebrows at me.

I held out my empty champagne flute and waited for him to fill it. He obliged and then set the bottle of champagne down and reached for his own flute. "To fake romance."

"Because the real kind never works." I smiled as I lifted my glass. "Cheers."

A few days before I met Jax at the bar, Mom and I had gone shopping in Great Barrington. She needed to find fabric for some new curtains. "It's a gorgeous house. Overlooks the cliffs. Antiques everywhere," she explained as we wound with the road into town. "The couple gave me full creative freedom. They only use the house for a few weeks a year over the summer and the occasional

Christmas party. They don't even want to be bothered — can you imagine?" She shook her head.

We couldn't imagine. That was never our life, to own a few extra homes. We'd brushed up against such things in the past and no doubt left the telltale marks of the bourgeoisie: the overly eager greeting, the dropped jaw.

That day Mom was wearing perfectly pressed white chinos, silver sandals that showed off her red toenails, and a crocheted sweater in an autumnal shade of orange. She wore her light-brown hair to her shoulders, her gray strands beat into submission with the help of regular coloring. The silver bracelets on her wrist clinked together as she pulled the car into a parking stall and tugged the emergency brake. She checked her watch. "I have to be quick. I'm meeting the girls for lunch. You know what they say: if you're late, you're a dollar short."

The center of Great Barrington is lined with little specialty shops and restaurants, places to buy stationery or handbags or to select a cheese-and-wine pairing for your next cocktail party. Mom avoided all of those stores and headed down a side street to Barrington Threads, which is the most expensive fabric store I have ever entered. Even if I sewed, I couldn't afford to make myself a pincushion from this material.

"'Morning, Dale!" she called out as she swept inside.

The elderly man stocking bolts of fabric on the shelf raised one hand. "Good morning, Mrs. Mallory!"

She'd never changed her last name after the divorce, and she still allowed people to refer to her as "Mrs." It struck me as oddly sentimental for someone who normally had no patience for such things. Mom operated in the world of the aesthetic: textures and colors and lighting. The emotional world had never interested her.

She stood in place, frowning down the rows. "I need blue. It has to be cerulean. And I was hoping to find a complementary damask." She looked this way and that before finally saying, "Let's try down here."

I was along for the ride and the company, except that I disappeared there in the fabric store. There was only my mom and the fabric. She slid her fingers along the threads, feeling for textures, checking them under different lights, holding paint samples against them. She liked to collect swatches. Half the time, she'd leave a store with nothing more than a collection of squares and possibilities. When I headed out on these errands with my mom, I ended up standing alone, watching her, feeling like an extra wheel.

"So I understand you're working with your father again?" She lifted one carefully sculpted brow at me. "How's that going?"

"Fine, I guess."

"And are you baking?"

"I'm on the coffee machine."

She paused to study a dark-blue fabric. Raw silk, if I had to guess. "Hmm. Your talents are wasted making coffee, Wren." She gave me a look. "If you're working in that bakery, you should at least be developing some useful skills. What is it they say about how it's better to teach someone to fish? It's the same with baking." She pulled the bolt of raw silk from the shelf and set it down. "I'm going to need a swatch of this."

"I don't like baking."

"That's just because you don't know how." She moved on to the next shelf and pulled a bolt of fabric from above her head. "This could work for the dining room. They have these lovely French doors and a lilac bush by a balcony. It's charming."

I drew a finger across a knobby light-blue material. "Have you seen the bakery lately?"

She released a long breath through her nostrils and returned the bolt in her hand to the shelf. "I'm not a breakfast person, honey. You know that. Just a cup of coffee for me."

"I don't mean that." I scratched at my ear and weighed my approach to the delicate discussion. "I was thinking that, you know, Dad hasn't changed the interior of the bakery for years. Ever, really. And I thought maybe you could swing by sometime and maybe help to give it an update." She continued with her review of the fabrics, and I wondered if she had heard me at all. "Mom?"

"It's awkward with me and your father. We've drawn certain boundaries." But she stopped, turned halfway to me. "Let me think about it."

It was the best I could hope for.

By the time we were finished, Mom had accumulated piles of bolts in various shades and textures of blue, and Dale had clipped swatches for her and attached them to little squares of card stock. "I'm going to have to sit with these later and come back tomorrow or Tuesday," Mom mused, as much to herself as to me. "I'm already running late for lunch."

"You're meeting them in Archer Cove?"

"Yes. I'll have just enough time to drop you off." She smiled and reached out to stroke my hair. "Too bad you don't enjoy interior design. I could use some help on a few new accounts I picked up last week."

"I'll stick to coffee," I said. "I'm getting better at it. When I finally move to the city, I can work as a barista and write on the side." This, I felt, would be an infinitely better option than sorting the mail, like I had in LA.

Mom sighed. "Your father should at least teach you a few recipes. He's just never been good at letting people in." She collected her bag of swatches. "Dale, it's always a pleasure. I'll probably see you tomorrow."

"Have a great day, Mrs. Mallory."

We headed back to the car, Mom's sandals clacking with each step as we swept past shops that I wished I had time to browse. "We'll have to come back," I said, pausing in front of a stationery store. I didn't have the money to buy expensive stationery, but I enjoyed the feel of paper and embossing.

"Absolutely." The lights to the car flashed and she opened the trunk remotely, dropped the bag inside, and clack-clacked to the driver's side. "We'll come back, and next time we'll have lunch."

Mom didn't have her interior design business, The Space Lift, when I was a child, but she used to perform some version of it on our house. It kept her busy when Dad was putting in all those hours on Wall Street. She made comforters and pillows, throws and curtains, seasonal table runners and napkins. She'd host the other mothers in the neighborhood for tea and sew new tablecloths and napkins for the occasion. Her favorite guests were Rosa Foley and Mickey.

One day as we sat on the perfectly green front lawn of her new mansion, Mickey informed me that I had fat ankles. "You can barely see them. See?" She held up one bare leg for me to admire. "I'm small boned. I have *slender* ankles."

I'd never thought about my ankles before. I mean, they worked just fine. It was sort of like noticing your liver. "So?"

"You'd probably never be able to model," she said. "*I* model. I'm in this year's Sears Christmas catalogue."

This is how it went. They'd come over for tea, or we'd drive into the city and shop at Bloomingdale's, and Mom and I would come away feeling a little bit flawed. Mom started paying more attention to her hairstyle and makeup, and she seemed to be on a perpetual diet. Still, she was happy. Being close to Rosa meant that Mom, the daughter of schoolteachers, had arrived somewhere. Dad was not as enthusiastic about the friendship.

"She's shallow, Lil," he said once as Mom recounted a shopping trip and Rosa's comments about the season's garish colors. "Her life is consumerism."

"You say that now, Hank," she replied with a laugh, "but wait until this summer. Rosa has a friend who has a place in the Hamptons. She says we can all stay there. For free."

Dad turned and walked out of the room rather than replying, and Mom smiled to herself, probably counting this as a victory. Then, weeks later, Dad quit his Wall Street job and declared he was going to buy a bakery in Archer Cove, a seaside town we'd visited a few times. He dropped this news on us one night when we were eating Chinese takeout.

"And where are we going to *live*?" Mom demanded. She had frozen, her empty chopsticks hovering in mid-air.

"There's an apartment above the bakery. Three bedrooms." Dad calmly took a sip of his water. "I'm done working eighty hours a week to subsidize everyone else's dreams. We can afford this, and it's the right time to make a change."

We packed the house and moved two months later. Mom lasted exactly eight days in that apartment before renting out a room at the Archer Cove Inn, where she plotted how she would create her own interior design business. She was going to live in Great Barrington, just in a little place for now, until she got The Space Lift off the ground. "The thing I have going for me is taste," she explained as she took a sip from her glass of ice water.

Inside floated two rounds of lemons. "I've always been good at this kind of thing, Wren. And it's time for me to work outside of the home. You're in middle school, and your father and I...we grew apart."

Mom didn't have room for me in her new apartment, so I lived with Dad, which suited me fine. At least with Dad, I knew that if he wasn't at home, he was in the bakery. Mom was more elusive, chasing something that required her to constantly move and shift, like a sparrow pestering a hawk.

Excerpt from Celebrity Burn, June 23
Posted by: Rubee

Poppy Hayes made quite a splash at the premier of A Night in Venice, *but not for the reasons you may think. The five-foot-ten blonde stunner looked almost unrecognizable with her line-free smile and pouty lips, but she has not admitted to undergoing surgery or receiving Botox injections. She wore her long hair in sexy loose waves and a side part and opted for natural makeup, choosing a fresh, glossy pink lipstick and a smidge of mascara. When asked about her new look, Poppy attributed her appearance to power yoga, healthy eating, drinking eight glasses of water a day, and regular colonics — a combination that she called "life altering." "Good health begins in the gut, so I'm trying to flush out all of the toxins that accumulate over the years and contribute to aging."*

Uh, thanks for sharing, Poppy, but that last part may be a bit too much information. And colonics have smoothed out your

57

wrinkles? Sure they have (wink wink). This blogger isn't ready to give up the search for that Botox receipt just yet.

CHAPTER THREE

JAX CALLED HIS publicist, Taryn, to tell her he was in love. She couldn't have been more pleased. "I love it," she said sharply, the way she said everything. "Be sure to send me your schedule and I'll notify the right people."

We were sitting in his suite. Jax was on the bed, lying back on the pillows stacked against the headboard. I was perched on one of the leather couches, my spine rigid, my ankles pressed together, my hands folded on my lap. *Like a complete tight-ass*, I realized, and shifted to toss one arm across the armrest so that I looked more like I wanted to be there, in the same room as a hot leading man. But to me, he was just a means to an end.

"What do you mean, our schedule?" Jax watched the cell phone in his hand while he spoke. He'd put Taryn on speaker. "I've already given you my —"

"Your schedule. When you're going to a restaurant. When you're going for a walk. And make sure you hold hands," Taryn added. "People love that."

"Ah." He glanced down and started to scratch at something on the comforter. "Got it."

"Tell her to be sure to obstruct her face," Taryn said. "Keep it mysterious. Is she there now? Tell her to do that."

Jax looked at me. "Taryn wants you to obstruct your face."

"Yeah, I heard. How am I supposed to do that?"

"What? Is she there? Is that her?" Taryn didn't wait for the response. "Make sure to tell her to get a wide hat. You know, one of those sun hats? A straw one would be cute. Wear her hair in her face. Keep her head down."

I folded my arms. "Maybe I should just wear a paper bag on my head."

He brought his hand up to his forehead and started rubbing it. I almost felt bad for him, having to deal with a publicist who barked at him like that. "What's that about, Taryn? Why does she need to hide her face?"

There was the sound of a car honking in the background. "Just tell her to obstruct her face, but not in an obvious way. Just create some mystery. Everyone will be dying to know what she looks like. Yeah, gimme a venti mocha soy latte, no whip. Jax? You still there?"

"Yeah. Still here."

"Does she have a name?"

Jax glanced at me. "I'd like to keep her name out of the press for now. She's a little...shy."

I threw a pillow at him, but missed.

"Whatever. Anyway, I think it's great you're in love, babe. Just make sure you sell it, okay? Make sure you're not seen with anyone else. *Capisce?*"

"Yep."

"And Jax? I'm assuming she's hot, babe. This isn't going to work with a plain Jane."

He met my gaze and then shifted. "Yeah. Okay."

"Gotta run. We'll talk. *Ciao.*"

He tossed the phone to the side of the bed. "Well, we have Taryn's blessing." He stretched out along the bed, reaching his muscular arms to the side.

"As long as no one sees my face." It stung, as did his failure to defend me from the "plain Jane" assault. I pulled a green throw pillow onto my lap and brought my knees up to my chest.

"She doesn't mean anything by it," Jax said, directing his words to the ceiling. "Isn't anonymity what you want? Our relationship should mostly consist of you heading up to my suite." He turned his head to grin. "It's the best kind of relationship, anyway."

"Please. I don't want to spend my life in this suite, sitting around while the paparazzi imagine we're...you know." A flush crawled up my cheeks.

Jax rolled onto his side. "We're what, Wren? Feeling each other up? Having sex?" He grinned. "Bonking each other mindless?"

My face was burning. I'd once had a therapist who assured me that I couldn't be held responsible for the thoughts that entered my mind, only for my response to them. God help me, but right then I was thinking about what it might be like to be one of the women Jax was actually attracted to, one of the many gorgeous, leggy women he'd taken home to, as he put it, "bonk."

Fine — I was wondering how he bonked. There, I said it. I couldn't help it, as he'd dangled the suggestion right in front of me. Dangled wasn't the right word. That made me think of his...forget it. I had to look away and change the subject.

"That's not the point," I said. "I don't want to spend all of my free time sitting around here."

He shot me a devilish smile. "We could always do what they imagine we're doing. Why waste the opportunity?"

"Has hell frozen over? Thanks anyway."

He shrugged and rolled onto his back again. "Can't say I didn't try."

"I still —"

"Bring a book, Wren. Play solitaire. Write one of your —" he waved a hand dismissively in my direction. "*Movies*. We're not talking about months of this, anyway. A few weeks, tops. Just enough time to enjoy the festival and attend a few parties." He turned his head. "That's still okay, right? You'll attend parties with me? Because I don't want to interfere with your social calendar. I'm sure it's burning up."

A smile pulled tightly across my face. "I can always find time for someone as charming as yourself." I glanced at the time. "I've been here for two hours. I can't imagine that you'd be able to perform that long. You know, since we're going for verisimilitude here."

"You might be surprised." Jax continued to stare at the ceiling, unaffected by the barb. "But lunch and a quickie works for me. Just make sure to wear the hat and keep your head down. We want people to think you're hot." He reached over to the nightstand, grabbed a remote control, and turned on the television. After flipping through a few channels, he landed on a soccer game.

I was already setting the hat on my head again, tucking my hair underneath. I finger combed some strands over my cheeks, feeling unkempt but better concealed. Then I slung my handbag over my shoulder. "So should we, uh, make plans to see each other again?"

"Afraid you might miss me, darling?" His mouth quirked into a rakish, one-sided grin. "We have the party on Friday. We'll be in touch before then."

"Right. Brennan's red carpet event." I thought through my clothing options. I was confident I didn't own a thing that I'd want to be caught dead wearing. "So, should I get a dress?"

"Oh good lord, no. I'll take care of that. And I'll have someone here to help you dress that night. I'll send a car by your place."

"Should I write down my address?"

He pointed to the desk in the corner. "I think there's a pen and paper there."

I thought about my little apartment, with all of its boxes still piled in the hallway and Crabby Andy's in the back, and paused to consider whether I could send Jax's "car" anywhere else. No, I couldn't.

I scribbled my address on the paper and set it aside. "There. Well. I guess I'll be seeing you."

"Yep."

His gaze was fixed on the soccer game as I walked toward the door, and while I realized the entire relationship was a farce, I couldn't help but feel a little disappointed. Shouldn't my willingness to go along with this charade inspire *some* kind of affection?

I closed the door gently behind me and hurried down the steps, not wanting to meet anyone in the hall. No. This was not about any kind of affection. This was about getting my work into the hands of a producer who could change my life. This fake relationship was about succeeding for real.

As I breezed through the reception area and into the summer evening, I vowed to get to work on that screenplay.

I returned to my apartment, brewed a pot of coffee, and set my laptop on my kitchen table, determined to write. I had been working on a screenplay for ages, but it never seemed quite right. I had the outline of changes in my mind, and I needed to get working on them before the threads were lost forever. The day was warm, so I opened the windows wide, allowing the gentle breeze to infuse my apartment with the scents of salt water and fried clams. As the coffee brewed, I watched a few cooks from Crabby Andy's congregate for a cigarette break beside the Dumpster. I frowned. The advertisement had promised me ocean views.

No matter. I could be inspired by anything. I could summon my muse at will, direct her to channel the great stories of the heavens through my body and down onto my keyboard. I helped myself to a mug of coffee, added a splash of cream, and sat before my keyboard. Today, I was going to address the time-traveling romance. I was just starting to get into a groove when there was a knock at the door.

I sighed and pushed back from the table. The movers had stacked the boxes on both sides of the hallway, so I had to turn sideways, scooting like a crab. When I opened the door, Jessie was standing there with a white cardboard box tied with a thin, blue-striped string. I recognized it instantly as coming from Hedda's, and I knew it would be filled with pastry. In her other hand was a bottle of champagne. "Hey, you," she beamed. "Happy housewarming. I thought I could help you unpack, if you want." Bless her industrious heart. She thrust the box and bottle into my arms. "Here. I brought muffins."

Her arrival made my heart sputter. I love my cousin, I do. It's just that I was trying to immerse myself in the

Roaring Twenties. I accepted the box of muffins and stepped aside to allow her entry. "Thanks. Actually, I was just sitting down to write —"

"What is that? It smells like...fish?" She wrinkled her nose.

"Yeah. That would be the fish place next door."

"Well." She shrugged and gave me that endlessly optimistic smile. "I'm sure it's only seasonal."

She was off without another word, reaching for the top box on the stack. It must have been light. She turned it over in her hands. "It looks like you forgot to mark this one."

I pulled at the end of my ponytail and looked away. In my haste to flee LA, I'd sort of neglected to mark *any* of the boxes. I'd convinced myself that I didn't have the time, and further justified it by thinking that unpacking would become an adventure. If I didn't mark the boxes, I'd never be sure whether the box I was opening would contain kitchen towels or the porcelain figurine of the boy in lederhosen Aunt Esther had given me one year. That would be kind of fun, right?

But Jessie wouldn't be convinced, and my reasoning wasn't sitting well with me, either. "I was in a hurry to leave," I said. "I didn't think about anything but getting out of there."

Her face scrunched with sympathy. "Of course you didn't, you poor thing. How about if I tackle these boxes? You go do whatever you were doing."

But I couldn't go sit at my keyboard to write about flappers while she unpacked my apartment, could I? "No, let me help you. Can I get you some coffee?"

"Sounds great." She had set the box on the floor and was ripping the packing tape from the seams.

I turned sideways and shuffled toward the kitchen. Once there, I got down to work, feeling like maybe this could become my new purpose in life, to make coffee for other people. *I am the coffee girl.* It sounded less superhero and more pinup. I had a friend in LA who specialized in pinup photography. You could create a calendar of yourself in all kinds of different poses and scenarios: a sexy auto mechanic, a sexy librarian, a sexy dog walker, you name it. Could she do a sexy barista? I'd have to ask.

My little coffee maker was downright elementary compared to the gadget Dad had at Hedda's, though. That one was loaded with different levers and buttons and required the use of a thermometer. This was a standard model: pour water, scoop coffee, press red button. I could do it half-asleep, which I suppose was kind of the point.

I poured a mug for Jessie and grabbed my own, shutting down my laptop. I'd have plenty of time to revise that screenplay later. I was sure there would be some lag time between the end of my fake romance with Jax and his opportunity to pass my work to the right hands. No harm done, and I needed to unpack eventually.

Jessie had already stacked piles of pillows and towels to the side and flattened the empty cardboard box. "You don't have too much here. It probably looks like more than it is."

"I love your optimism." I handed her the mug. "I also love you for making me unpack."

"You shouldn't have to do this all alone," she said. "I mean, look at this stack of boxes. What if one fell on you?" She shook her head. "No. This is what family is for."

We were sort of having a Moment, where I was feeling like she was the one person in the world who understood that my refusal to unpack was not due to laziness. There was no need to go and muck it up with a verbal response, so I reached for the next box — which was quite heavy — and set it on the floor. Ah, here were my books!

We'd created a nice system and had brought the stacks down to waist height when Jessie suddenly burst into tears. "Oh. Oh my gosh." I rushed to embrace her. "What happened? Did something fall on you?"

She accepted my shoulder and wrapped her arms tightly around me, squeezing me back. When she'd caught her breath, she said, "We have to sell Hedda's."

My knees went limp. I took a step back, still clutching her arms. "Wait. Did I hear you correctly?"

"Your dad and I talked about it this afternoon. Business is down, and the cost of everything is rising. We've kept it going for as long as we could, but there's no choice." She swept her fingers across her damp cheeks. "Sorry. Did we unpack tissues yet?"

My body reeled as I backed away. "I'll get you some."

Selling the bakery. My heart had dropped out of my chest and gone skittering across the floor. What would my dad do? What would Jessie do? I walked to the bathroom on legs that felt like jelly, retrieved a box of tissues, and came back. "Gosh, Jess. I'm so damn sorry." I swallowed a lump in my throat.

"Thanks." She accepted the box and sat on the floor, leaning her back against the wall. She blew her nose. "I guess I shouldn't be surprised. That's why I was doing this catering business, you know? I thought it could make some extra money to support the bakery, but with the start-up costs...All of that work, and it hasn't made any difference at all."

I lowered myself to the floor beside her and wrapped my arms around my knees. Of course I knew that selling the bakery meant I would be out of a job, too, but at that moment all I could think was that Jessie was the kindest, sweetest person I'd ever met, and that this was her dream the same way writing was mine. I wasn't about to sit by and do nothing.

At my insistence, we left my apartment and went to Dad's house. He'd only purchased his own place in the last five years — a modest white ranch a few miles from the bustle of the town center. His face lit up when he opened the door to see us standing on the front step. "Hey, buttercup!" He pulled me into a hug and gave me a kiss on the cheek. "And Jessie. Hi, honey." He gave her a kiss and a hug as well. "I was just about to cook dinner. Want to stay? I'm just grilling some burgers."

"Sure, Dad," I said.

"Come on in."

I tried not to stare at him as he opened the door wide to allow us through. I'd always considered him handsome in a dad kind of way. He had an honest, demonstrative face, the kind that didn't mind being read by others. He was smiling, but I could see the tension in the way his shoulders sat a little higher, the lines on his forehead grew a little deeper. He closed the door behind us, and I turned to face him. "Dad, Jessie told me about the bakery."

"Oh." He recovered quickly and set a hand on my shoulder. "I don't want you to worry about that. I'm going to take care of you. Both of you." A little squeeze, and he walked into the kitchen.

Jessie and I exchanged a glance. "Dad. There's got to be something we can do. You know, with the film festival in town, maybe we could run a promotion? I know some people." Maybe Jax would be willing to make an appearance at the bakery, to sign autographs and pose for pictures. It was the least he could do, considering I was pretending to sleep with him.

"Honey, believe me. I've put up a good fight. So has Jessie." He opened the refrigerator and started to place items on the counter: ketchup and mustard, a jar of pickles. "I'm going to get the best price I can for us. For you, Wren. I'm going to repay you."

"Repay me? For what?"

"Don't you remember? Oh, don't feel bad. You were just a kid." He grabbed a plate of raw hamburger patties from the refrigerator and closed the door with one foot. "It was part of the divorce settlement. You're half owner of the building. So really, once we sell, you're going to have some money coming back."

"Wait." My legs went weak again, and a sidelong glance at Jessie's open mouth told me she was learning something new, too. "Wait. I'm part owner of the bakery?"

"Of the building, yes. A sale means we'll be liquidating some assets. You can use that money to do what you want. It's not enough to buy a house, but it's enough that you won't have to worry about money for a while. Hey, Jessie," he pointed to a wooden bowl on the kitchen table. "Can you hand me that, hon? Thanks."

A little slow on the uptake, I had to swirl that information around my noggin for a moment while dad washed a head of iceberg lettuce. Selling the bakery meant that he and Jessie would be out of jobs, but I would be collecting a fat payday? "Dad, that's horrible," I blurted out. "If I'm half owner, then I don't want to sell." I folded my arms. "How's that?"

"Calling you half owner was a little generous on my part," he said calmly. "You own forty-nine percent. And anyway, it's all part of your trust. I have to act in your best interest, which means that I have to sell the business. If we hold on any longer, we risk losing everything."

"It's possible another bakery will buy it, Wren," Jessie said. "Who knows? Maybe the only thing that changes is the ownership, and a few months from now we're all still working together."

God, her optimism. I had to admire it as she stood there next to my dad, slicing tomatoes, but right then it felt like I was the only one capable of facing this reality head-on.

Hedda's was more than a bakery and my family's livelihood. It was where I'd grown up. I'd recovered from my show business heartache in that kitchen, done my homework with a slice of cinnamon toast at those tables. I loved that bakery. "What happened?" I forced the question out around the lump that was forming in my throat.

He met my gaze, and his eyes were sad. "The usual. Increasing costs. Competition."

"Paris Street Sweets is opening in a few weeks," Jessie said. "They sell cupcakes the size of small babies."

"They're well-capitalized," Dad added. "They're going to try to undercut us at every opportunity."

"Is that what it is? Paris Street Sweets?" I threw my hands up helplessly. "Well, that hasn't even happened yet! We can talk about new — you know, places to buy flour and sugar."

"Wholesalers," Jessie said.

"Yes. Wholesalers. Maybe we could find cheaper ones. And with the catering business, maybe we can branch out and offer a delivery service of some kind."

Dad was watching me as I rambled on, sharing my big ideas that admittedly had no basis in reality. I was the coffee girl, and I was trending barely competent at that. What did I know about saving a bakery business? When I took a breath and looked at him, I saw the pity. He knew it all, and he felt the same way I did.

I swallowed. "Don't look at me like that." My voice cracked. "I'm trying to help you."

"Tell you what," he said. "Let's have dinner. When we're done, I'll let you look at the books, and if you have any ideas, I want to hear them."

"Dad, I —"

"It's not what I want to do, Wren." He pinched his lips tightly and shook his head. "Believe me."

I let it drop. I had nothing to add to the conversation, anyway.

As promised, Dad let me inspect the books after dinner. I had him explain the columns to me, and it took me a few minutes to orient myself, but then I saw it. He was right. The margins were razor thin, and lately they'd disappeared entirely. It wasn't a matter of pushing more cinnamon rolls. Something big needed to happen.

I went home that night and finished most of my unpacking by myself, weeping. All these years I'd owned half of that bakery, and they had to sell it to protect my investment. My stomach ached.

I fell asleep around midnight, fully clothed and on top of my mattress. The alarm went off at four thirty, but I didn't even grumble when I hit the shower. That day, I had a new purpose. I was going to save that bakery. For once, I was not going to be responsible for dragging anyone down with me.

I'd experienced a string of failures in my life. Relationships. Careers. But this? This was something I was going to succeed at.

CHAPTER FOUR

JAX AND I were striving for realism, so we hit the usual date places: an ice cream parlor, a hot dog stand, the quaint shops in the center of Great Barrington. The blogs called us "adorable" with an exclamation point, and looking at the photos, we really were kind of a cute pair. I guess it helped that I had achieved virtual expertise at concealing half of my face from the cameras. As a couple, we were a gorgeous male actor and the suggestion of a beautiful brunette. My actual looks were much more modest.

The thing about a fake relationship is that it sort of begins to feel real after a while. We held hands while taking a stroll down Arrow Beach. We had coffee at a table so small our knees touched. Jax was so committed to staring longingly into my eyes when the cameras were around that it was all beginning to mess with my head.

"Say something funny," he said as we headed to the black Maserati he'd rented. We were walking with our fingers intertwined loosely, three photographers trailing us. The dark hair on his forearm tickled my skin.

"What, like a knock knock joke?" I searched my memory. "You know I don't think well on my feet like this."

But it didn't matter, because he burst into laughter like I was the funniest person ever. "You should write that stuff down, turtle," he said, shaking his head.

Turtle. Yes, he was throwing around ridiculous pet names. I'd elected to refer to him as food items. "I'm overcompensating. One of us has to be funny, cookie," I said. When we reached the car, he took the shopping bags from my hands and opened my door. "Why, thank you, wheat puff."

He smirked. "Don't mention it, my little scorpion."

He shut the door, and I waited with my face down while he walked to the driver's side. The routine was always the same: he picked me up at a designated spot several blocks away from my apartment, we drove somewhere for a "date," and then he dropped me off somewhere else, leaving me to walk home alone. This way, I'd maintain my privacy and anonymity. So far, so good.

"Taryn says that the relationship is reading well," he said as he backed away from the parking stall. "Her words." He shifted the car into gear and we were off. Jax liked fast cars. "Public opinion of me is rising now that I'm in love."

"Oh, is that according to the latest scientific poll?"

I took off my straw hat and shoved it into the shopping bag, which was strictly a prop. We were in the clear now. I'd left my bike in a remote area on the outskirts of town, hidden under a pile of leaves. Honestly, the things I'd do to sell a screenplay.

"You can joke all you want, Wren," he replied, downshifting at a sharp curve in the road. "This fake relationship has done wonders for my very real career."

"I'm so glad to hear that, Jax. I've found it rewarding to be your fake girlfriend this week. I can only hope our relationship destructs in a publicly monumental manner."

"Yeah, we're going to have to do some thinking about that one. You know, plan some dates where things between us are looking tense. You might want to practice looking sullen."

"I can sell sullen. Believe me."

"It's not going to be until after the party," he said. "I need this to last a little longer, maybe fizzle out slowly. I've told Taryn that we were old friends. She's going to float that to a few reporters. I thought it added some depth to the relationship."

"Sure. But in fairness, this relationship is pretty shallow." I took a sip from the bottle of water that Jax insisted I carry with me on all dates. "When is Brennan supposed to make a decision about the role of Ben, anyway?"

Since I'd learned of the bakery's financial troubles, my focus was laser-like. The sooner Jax was cast as Ben, the sooner my screenplay would land on Brennan's desk, and the sooner he would make an offer I couldn't refuse and I could use all of my proceeds to save the bakery. The possibility may have been thin, but it was all I had.

"My agent says it's any day now. Once the ink on that deal is dry, we can break up." He slowed as we approached the area where I'd left my bike, and pulled to the side of the road.

"Thanks for the ride. I had a thoroughly acceptable time this afternoon." I unfastened my seatbelt.

"Good," he said. "I'll send my driver by your place to pick you up tomorrow afternoon, before the party. I won't make you bike to the woods again."

"And they say chivalry is dead." I shut the door behind me.

He waited as I made my way to the ditch where I'd hidden my chariot: an old purple ten-speed that Dad bought for me on my twelfth birthday. The gears were a little rusty, but at least it didn't come with a basket. I pulled an elastic cord from the bottom of the shopping bag and secured the bag to the back, behind the seat, before giving Jax a little wave. "See you tomorrow."

"Hey." Jax poked his head out of the window. "I realize you have some hang-up about prostitution, but I insist on buying you a new bicycle."

"What's wrong with this one?" I couldn't help but feel a little injured.

He winced. "It makes me think of orphaned children."

"It works just fine." I sat on the seat and managed to get in two pumps of the pedals before the chain broke.

I dismounted and tried to piece the chain together, but then I had not only a broken bike chain, but grease all over my fingers. "Dammit." It was a little over three miles home.

Behind me, I heard Jax open the door of the Maserati and sigh. I braced myself for a snide remark. "It's fine. I don't need help. This happens all the time." Without a word, he calmly lifted the bicycle from the road and carried it toward the car. "Wh-what are you doing?"

"Putting it out of its misery."

He moved quickly, popping the front tire from the frame and stashing the entire bicycle in the trunk. It was quite impressive, actually. "Come on. Get in."

I looked down at my hands. "I'm covered in grease."

He paused halfway as he climbed inside the car, throwing a sexy smirk over his shoulder. "You're also covered in polyester. Get in the car."

He waited for me to open the passenger side door and fasten my seatbelt before he shut the door and turned the key in the ignition. I watched him fuss with the air conditioning and the vents, noting the way he'd rolled his shirt sleeves to his elbow. "Comfortable?" he asked.

"Yes," I mumbled, even though I wasn't at all. I was oddly flushed by the unexpected kindness. "Thank you. You don't have to do this."

He stopped to type something into his phone, adjusted the rearview mirror, and then set off down the road, jerking me back into my seat. "Your bicycle is broken. What did you think I'd do, speed away?"

I folded my hands together and set them demurely on my lap, not wanting to touch anything in the gorgeous leather interior. "I guess I never expected you to go all knight in shining armor on me. I mean, not for a fake relationship."

"I'm not a complete monster." He eyed me sidelong. "Are you in a hurry? I was planning to make a stop."

"Oh! By all means. Please do." The only things on my to-do list that night were to work on my screenplay and eat ice cream. Important, but Jax was giving me a ride, and there was no need to be rude.

"Great."

He didn't elaborate or give any hint as to our destination. His jaw was set, his gaze focused on the drive ahead. The windows were rolled down, so there was no opportunity to talk. Just as well, since something about him had left me tongue-tied. Maybe this was the "je ne sais quoi" people in the business talked about, that magnetism that movie stars possessed. Maybe it was the intoxicating blend of fast car and rakish man, or maybe I had low blood sugar. As we zipped down the road, the ocean beating its pulse to our right, I pondered the pickle I was in. Blushing and folding my hands in my lap? I couldn't remember the last time I'd done that around a man. Not even Griff. I reminded myself to be a professional.

A professional what?

"Have you guessed where we're going yet?" Jax shouted over the wind gusting through the windows. "I'll give you a hint: it's about you."

"Me?" My heart jumped. I pressed my hands together more firmly and felt the grit and grease shift across my skin. "You're not getting me breast implants, are you?"

"No." He allowed me to observe his gaze dipping below my neckline. "They look fine to me."

Eyes back on the road, and just great. My skin was burning at this point. I had stopped worrying about Jax turning out to be a serial killer. Wouldn't that be an odd twist on things? But no, it didn't cross my mind as we drove to this secret place that was somehow about me that maybe he was planning to deposit my body in the woods. Besides, I knew we were in Spencer, two towns over from Archer Cove. I relaxed slightly. Rookie mistake.

The car slowed and pulled onto the main street. I'd been here before, of course, but never for long. I'd always assumed that people who shopped in Spencer could smell the Archer Cove working class in me. My pulse kicked a little as the car continued down a line of shops before stopping in front of *Belle Tique*. A woman in a dove-gray sheath dress and a strand of glossy pink pearls that matched her heels was waiting for us. "Mr. Cosgrove," she gushed as Jax opened the door. "Such a pleasure, sir. I'm Annie. I own *Belle Tique*."

"Annie." Jax leaned forward to give her a kiss on the cheek. "I've brought my friend with me today."

My hands went clammy. *Belle Tique*? *This* was the surprise? I swallowed and nudged open my door, trying not to sully the leather with bike grease. Jax rushed over to help, fortunately. By the time I got to my feet, I swear my bones where shivering.

Jax, on the other hand, was all smiles. "Annie. This is Wren."

I searched his face helplessly for a clue, and to avoid watching Annie's appraisal. I was covered in grime and, as Jax had noted, polyester. She was the owner of a clothing boutique that carried shoes that cost more than my monthly rent. "No fair," I whispered, rising up on my toes to deliver it straight into his ear. "Are you trying to make fun of me?"

Surprise dashed across his face, followed by concern. "No. Not at all. I was here the other day and I thought of you."

A wave of humiliation threatened to bubble to the surface, and I blinked back the tears. "Jax, I swear, if you're doing this to laugh at me —"

"Wren. So nice to meet you, honey." Annie coaxed an arm behind my back and ushered me to the sidewalk. "Oh, look at your hands! Let's get you cleaned up."

We stepped into the boutique and a young saleswoman greeted us with a smile and then promptly locked the door behind us. VIP treatment. "Casey, hon," Annie called over her shoulder. "Be a doll and get me a warm towel and some lemon water."

"We went for a walk," Jax explained, "and Wren ran into someone with a broken bicycle. She fixed it herself."

"Aren't you lovely?" Annie gasped at my side. "I swear, I've never been mechanically inclined, myself. Now, give me a sewing machine and a potato sack, and I'll give you a dress. But I wouldn't know the first thing about fixing a bicycle."

I glanced at Jax for help, because of course I didn't know the first thing about fixing a bicycle, either. He was studying a case of jewelry and didn't notice. "It — it wasn't very heroic," I managed. "Just a slipped chain."

Casey had appeared with a hot, wet towel that Annie used to swab at my dirty hands. It smelled faintly of lemon. "I'm sure you're being modest," Annie said. "There. Your hands are clean and you're ready to shop." She set the towel back on a silver tray, which Casey silently carried out of sight.

I glanced around the shop. *Belle Tique* carried Annie's original designs: shimmering cocktail dresses and matching handbags, elegant business attire, and unique accessories. She also carried high-end designer lines, Versace and Vera Wang, and many names I didn't recognize. I had read a few reviews of her boutique, but I'd never been brave enough to set foot inside. "I — I guess I'll browse," I muttered. There was no way I could afford a single item in here, I was certain.

"Feel free," Jax said casually as he came up beside me. "But I helped Casey to select a few items that I thought you might like."

"I understand you need a gown," Annie said. "Casey selected some for you to try on."

"I'll wait here." Jax took a seat in a leather armchair that faced the dressing room and crossed one ankle over his knee.

My jaw was open, and I'd barely registered what was happening when Casey tugged me into a dressing room. "We weren't sure of your size," she said with a grin, and lowered her voice. "Men. Am I right? But I have to say, Mr. Cosgrove has excellent taste." She stood back and gave me a once-over. "I'm going to grab a few things for you to try on. You can start undressing."

She vanished, leaving me standing in a large room with three mirrors. I caught a glimpse of myself, and my stomach lurched. My brown hair was windblown and snarled, and I looked ashen under the glare of the lights. I turned toward the blue silk curtain, trying to avoid any glimpse of my own bare skin as I slid out of my definitely not-designer clothing. My pants were smudged with grease. Still, I folded them as carefully as if they had cost me a fortune and set them on a little padded bench.

"Here we are," chirped Casey, pulling a rack of clothing behind her. She pushed her chin-length auburn hair behind her ears and started sliding the hangers around. "He says you like dresses. Is that right?"

I thought of the sundress I'd worn to his room at the inn. Why was I so surprised that he'd remembered? "Yes. I do."

"You'll love this, and it's a nice shade of blue. It will bring out your eyes."

She helped me into a sheath dress that slid like silk down my skin. The fabric was cool to the touch, and soft. "Nice, isn't it?" Casey smiled as she smoothed the skirt in place. "I thought this would fit. After working in a boutique, one of my superpowers is that I can usually tell someone's size instantly." She stepped back. "Well? Let's show him."

The blood rushed to my feet. "What? Show...Jax?"

"They love the show, trust me." Casey winked. "Go on. He's going to lose his mind when he sees you in that. It's totally sexy."

My hand fumbled for the scooped neckline, and I wondered how much more of this I'd have to endure. When Jax had asked me to be his fake girlfriend, I should've made him iron out more details. Clothing shopping and a miniature fashion show was *so* not me. I took a breath as she lifted the curtain for me to walk through, then I stepped uncertainly down to where Jax and Annie were chatting. As I approached, they both stopped. Jax smiled. "Wow."

I glanced down at my bare feet. "Is that a good 'wow'? Or more like, 'Wow, you'd better get out of that before the designer sees you desecrating her creation'?"

He chuckled. "A good 'wow.' You look great."

He was sitting back in the leather chair, his legs splayed widely, as he watched. Casey was right, he *did* seem to be enjoying himself, but not in the mean-spirited way I'd feared. More like a genuine way, which only set a fire blazing across my skin.

Jax turned to Annie. "We're going to take that."

She nodded. "Of course. I'll have it wrapped."

He smiled at me. "Go on. Try on everything else. We're going to take everything you like."

The smile hardened on my face. "Jax. Maybe we should talk about this?"

"Nothing to talk about. I like to spoil my girlfriend. It's all my treat." He turned back to Annie. "Why don't you pick out some shoes for her, too. Maybe earrings."

"Of course."

I could see that the topic was closed, at least as long as Annie was hovering at his side. So this was part of the act, then? Just more of Jax sweeping his girlfriend off her feet? I teased the fabric of the dress between my fingers as I headed back to the dressing room, trying to ignore the disappointment that bloomed below my sternum. This wasn't real. None of it was. I'd do well to remember that.

Casey held the curtain open for me. "I told you he'd love it," she said.

"Yes."

I stole a glance in the mirror. The dress *was* gorgeous, and it really was something I'd enjoy wearing. The cut was flattering, and the shade of deep blue made my skin look smooth. I chewed on my lower lip. Honestly, this would all be finished in a week or so. May as well enjoy it while it lasted. "You know, Casey? I'd love to see what you have for sandals. Maybe a necklace and some bracelets, as well. And a matching handbag, too."

Casey nodded. "I'll be right back."

I smiled at my reflection. If Jax was going to play this game, then I was, too.

By the time we left *Belle Tique*, we had amassed six large shopping bags. I had a new summer wardrobe, essentially, except no one I knew could see me in any of it because I was trying to remain anonymous. "You hated my clothes that much?" I said as we fastened our seat belts. I was wearing the blue dress home, complete with five silver bracelets that clattered on my wrist and sexy leather sandals that made me glad I'd recently splurged on a pedicure.

"I wanted to do something nice for you," he said. "Is that a crime?"

"You should've just told me the truth. All of those comments about polyester." I tried to keep the hurt from creeping into my voice. Failed. "You know I don't have millions of dollars. I don't see how it's at all fair —"

"Wren." He slipped his hand over mine, stilling my thoughts. "I wanted to do something nice for you. That's all. I swear it."

My mind had gone blank. I nodded. "Okay."

"Good, then. Enjoy." He turned the key in the ignition and we sped down the road. "You know how much sex this entitles me to, right? I mean, just that dress alone — ow!" He jerked back his arm and laughed after I hit him square in the bicep. "I'm kidding!"

"Tell me, do those jokes work *ever*?" But I struggled not to laugh as he rubbed his arm. I'd barely touched him.

"I wouldn't even need to try jokes or shopping sprees with most women. You should consider yourself lucky."

But I didn't feel lucky as we returned to Archer Cove and I realized the shopping bags would force me to give Jax my actual address rather than asking him to drop me off somewhere else. I felt sick as I helped him navigate to my little two-family building beside the municipal park. "Thanks for the ride," I said.

I hoped no one at Crabby Andy's was watching me climb out of a Maserati. Good lord, I hoped my landlord wasn't home. What would she imagine I was doing to pay the rent?

Jax unfastened his seatbelt. "I'll get your bags."

"No, it's fine —"

"I insist."

I waited on the sidewalk while he lifted the bags from the trunk and waited expectantly. "Well? I'll carry them up."

"What? No. *No*." I reached for the shopping bags. "I can't. I think — my apartment's a mess, and there's some weird stain on the carpet, and maybe my cousin is there and waiting for me." The excuses came fast and furious.

"I can handle your cousin. You're the one who insists on being anonymous."

"Because of the bakery." I feared that the attention and gawking crowds would only drive our loyal customers away. "Besides, you don't know my cousin. She keeps a dead fox beside her door."

"Let me walk the bags up the stairs at least."

"No." I pried his fingers open and pulled the bags into my own hands. "Thank you. It's nice of you to offer. But no thank you."

I tried to decipher his furrowed brow. It looked oddly like disappointment. "Suit yourself. Don't say I never offered."

"Yes, you're great." It wasn't sarcastic. "It's me, okay? I have weird hang-ups about strange men in my apartment."

"And accepting gifts from those men. But I've made headway there." He shrugged. "You have issues. I always find the girls with issues."

"Well that explains everything. I hope you take my insurance, Dr. Cosgrove."

He rubbed at his forehead with his free hand. "You really are a special breed. I take you out for a fun afternoon and you reward me with sarcasm. This imaginary relationship is going to land us in couples' therapy before long."

I tilted my head at him. "I promise you don't need to worry about my issues or offer to pay for my therapist."

"Good thing, because I'm just about broke after this afternoon's detour to *Belle Tique*." Jax frowned. "But I don't understand you, Wren. How does dating a movie star hurt your family's bakery? I'd think it would boost business. I'm not going to lie — it feels a bit personal."

I glanced down at my new sandals, so pretty even against the steely gray concrete of the sidewalk. "You're right, you *don't* understand. You actually like it when people gawk at you."

"So I'm right. It's not really about the business." He slipped his finger under my chin and raised my eyes to meet his. "What's going to happen at the party on Friday? You're going to have to come out as yourself eventually. It's part of the arrangement."

"I know," I said, reaching up to take his hand. "I'll resolve my issues by then. Okay?"

Somehow our fingers interlaced, and we stood there for a moment staring at each other before I realized how intimate it all was. I allowed his hand to drop. Yes, I was playing a part, but I didn't need to be foolish about it.

If Jax sensed my discomfort, he didn't let on. "Fine. I'll leave." He sighed and stepped off the sidewalk. "And I'm keeping your piece of shit bicycle. If I manage to sell it for scrap I'll split the profits with you, sixty-forty."

"You're so sweet, Jax. See you at the party."

I watched as he drove away, standing on wobbly legs, not exactly sure what had just happened. Then I headed to the back of the building, where I could take the outdoor staircase. A guy from Crabby Andy's was tossing a large black trash bag into the Dumpster. He grinned at me and gave a whistle. "Lookin' good, mama."

I gritted my teeth as I climbed the stairs, feeling his eyes on me. I'd have to start using the front entrance.

CHAPTER FIVE

Excerpt from Celebrity Burn, June 29
Posted by: Rubee

Hollywood has officially infected Archer Cove, bringing life in the normally sleepy seaside town to a fever pitch. Tonight is the party everyone has been waiting for: famed producer Hodges Brennan's annual fete-to-end-all-fetes, located at his fourteen-bedroom summer home in the hamlet of Great Barrington. One never knows what they will encounter at a Brennan party, but last year's swag bag was worth thousands of dollars, and highlights included monogrammed diamond bracelets from Tiffany and gift certificates for a stay at a local spa.

Everyone who's anyone will be there, and yours truly will be bringing you the official scoop. I'm especially looking forward to sneaking a peek at Jax Cosgrove's mysterious lady friend. Sources say she may be The One who reforms his bad-boy image, but I'm going to be the judge of that.

BREATHING WAS THE most difficult thing. My corset was at least one size too small, and Lucian, my stylist, had pulled it to the tightest setting. "It hurts," I'd gasped. "My ribs feel like they're being pinched."

"But now you'll fit into the gown, my dear."

Lucian stepped back triumphantly and reached for the steel-blue Valentino. I lifted my arms to allow the fabric to cascade over my body. He then set to work pinching, smoothing, and pinning. Finally he stepped away. "Gorgeous," he declared. "Stunning. Wait until he sees you in *that*."

Lucian knew I was a fraud. Jax had called him in confidence and asked for his assistance to make me look presentable at Brennan's party. Photographers would be there, and while hiding might work when strolling along the beach, tonight the world would see my face. Lucian changed my body with a corset, styled my uncooperative hair into soft waves, and worked magic with his makeup brushes. When I looked in the mirror, I hardly recognized myself. After all, every inch of the person staring back at me from the mirror had been tweaked and modified in some way. "It's amazing," I whispered. "Lou, you're a genius."

He was a middle-aged, sinewy man with light blond, almost white hair and clear blue eyes. When he spoke, he still bore traces of his native Italian. He clasped my hands in his and gave me a kiss on each of my cheeks. "You are gorgeous, love," he said. "Have a lovely time."

I gathered the folds of my dress in my hands and started to head out toward the sitting area of the suite, where Jax was waiting. Lucian clicked his tongue behind me and darted to take the gown from my hands. "Let me help you."

"Thanks. It's just that this train is long —"

"I'll hold it for you."

So we walked like that into the suite, me in front, teetering on my silver stiletto heels that were a little too small, and Lucian behind me, holding my gown. Deep breaths were impossible, so I took a shallow breath before I opened the door, trying to ease the pinch at the pit of my stomach. I told myself that Jax's approval didn't matter. We weren't *really* dating, and how could I possibly compete with the gorgeous women who'd gone before me? Still, I wanted him to think I was beautiful. I wanted to see that approval in his eyes.

I opened the door and turned my head, looking for him. Then I heard it, the intake of breath. He came over to me from the balcony, dressed in a tuxedo with a gray vest. His dark hair was slicked back, and his cheeks were freshly shaved. He smelled nice, and a thrill darted up my spine as his gaze raked across my body. "Wren. You look stunning."

My fingers flew to one of the diamond chandelier earrings. "You too."

Then he frowned. "Be careful with the earrings. I have them on loan, so —"

And just like that, the cold splash of reality. I dropped my hand. "Of course. I'll return them."

The frown remained on his face, but he took my hand in his. "The driver is waiting."

There was a crowd gathered around the limousine, snapping pictures. Was this how it was to be someone like Jax? He leaned over to whisper in my ear, "Smile, darling."

But I couldn't smile. All I could do was keep my head down as we entered the limousine and stare, my heart pounding, as we finally drove away.

I will say this for Jax: he was committed to his role as my fake boyfriend. As we made our way through the crowd at the party, he held my hand or draped an arm around my waist. He must have sensed my anxiety because he'd relay funny stories about the guests to put me at ease. Sometimes it felt real — as real as anything like that can feel to an outsider.

Hodges Brennan had set his party in a Georgian-style revival mansion on the cliffs. Inside the house was a massive entertaining space with a stone fireplace and a black grand piano that transitioned easily to a slate patio overlooking the sea. Guests breezed inside and outside as they mingled, and gloved waiters bustled around us, nearly invisible as they offered champagne or hors d'oeuvres.

"You look tense," Jax said as he accepted something offered by a waiter and handed it to me. "Have an oyster. They're an aphrodisiac, you know."

I wrinkled my nose at the half shell he held out. "Ugh. No reason for that."

He lifted his shoulders nonchalantly. "If you want, I'll take you somewhere private. I'll bet I could loosen you up in fifteen minutes."

I'd almost become accustomed to Jax's blunt sexual advances, but something about this time was different. This time, the suggestion sent a bolt across my skin. "Okay. Let's go." Sometimes my mouth moves and there is no brain to back it up.

"Seriously?" His eyebrows arched sky-high. He set the oyster on a roving waiter's empty tray. "I thought I'd never get you to actually agree to it."

"Yes. I mean no. I'm not. I'm just kidding." Quick recovery, if a little awkward, and my cheeks were burning. "And I'm not even your type."

"It's not nice to tease." He wrapped one arm behind my waist and pulled me against him, bending forward until his lips tickled my ear. "I'd give you the ride of your life. Think about that."

I *was* thinking about it. All the time, in fact, and that had become a giant problem. Jax was consuming my thoughts the way a real boyfriend would, and everything about us was fiction. In a few days, a few weeks, tops, I'd be back to my completely ordinary life, albeit with a closetful of new clothes. Still.

I pressed my arms against the wall of his chest, trying to put some distance between us. "Thanks for the generous offer."

He smiled wickedly, his blue eyes intent on my mouth. Then, without warning, he kissed me. His lips were warm and soft. Deliciously skilled. As he pulled away, I wondered if it was foolish not to take him up on his offer. A gorgeous movie star wanted to have no-strings-attached sex with me. Maybe I should just dive off that cliff? The warmth of his mouth lingered on mine, leaving me momentarily breathless. Jax was breathless, too.

I stepped back and gave a casual smile that belied the emotional current threatening to break the surface. "Like I said. Thanks for the offer. If you'll excuse me for a moment."

The energy was so high that I couldn't stop shaking, and I made my way across the room, trying to get anywhere else, anywhere with air. The room was crowded and much too warm, and I had to turn my body this way and that to escape. I had to find someplace to hide, just for a few minutes. I made a beeline for the powder room and shut the door behind me.

Quiet. I could have stayed in there forever, with its lovely black granite counters and the expansive mirrors. I took a seat on a black chaise in the corner and felt my muscles melt against the leather.

"I haven't seen you before," the only other woman in the room said in a voice like warm honey. She was seated before the mirror, swirling a fluffy powder brush across her face. Her hair was dyed a light shade of red and pulled into a chignon that was secured at the top with a gaudy rhinestone barrette.

Maybe they weren't rhinestones. Probably not, knowing this crowd.

"It's my first time," I said.

"*Oh.*" She glanced back at me over her shoulder, her voice heavy with meaning. "Honey, you gotta pull yourself together. The party's just getting started."

I sat up straighter, feeling self-conscious. "What do you mean? Do I look —?" I rose and headed to the mirror to check my face

"Yes, you 'look,' all right," she laughed. "You look like you're about to lose your caviar. What's the matter, don't like crowds?" She twirled the powder brush into a compact and took another pass at her face.

"Not really." She was right, I did look a little pale, even under all of that makeup. I gestured to the seat beside her. "Mind if I sit?"

"I'd love it if you did." She dusted her nose and then glanced at me sidelong. "You came with Jax Cosgrove, didn't you?"

"Yes."

"I knew it." She snapped the compact shut and reached into a pink bag to retrieve a tube of mascara. I recognized it as a brand that I could only dream about affording. "You've got to tell me, honey: is he all that he's said to be?"

"I'm sorry?"

She made a fluttering sound from her throat and turned to face me straight on. "I've heard he's blessed in the manhood department. He can go for hours, something about meditation. Am I right? Oh, never mind." She patted me on the thigh and giggled. "You're probably much too polite to kiss and tell. I wish you would, though."

I adjusted my dress and straightened my necklace, neither of which needed adjustment or straightening, just to have something to do other than to sit there and stare at the complete stranger who wanted to know about my sex life with Jax. "Things are, uh, fine," I muttered.

"You know, I just have to ask. Does he wax his twig and berries? Because I've heard he's bare *everywhere*."

"I don't — I haven't —" She was staring at me so intently that I had to look away, and I caught a glimpse of my scorchingly hot face in the mirror. I bit my lower lip, then said, "I'm sorry, I don't feel comfortable discussing my boyfriend's genitals with you."

Her penciled eyebrows shot upward. "Really? Most women love to do a little braggy-brag about the hot bodies they're banging."

Oh heavens. I started to get up to leave, but then I remembered that kiss. Jax was using every arrow in his quiver on me. I might as well respond in my own way.

"All right. Fine." I turned toward her and leaned in. "That rumor wasn't true. Until I met him. Then, I insisted on it."

Her mouth pinched in delight, and her blue eyes widened. "You made him wax."

"I did." I nodded. "The whole thing. We went to this little place I know and got matching Brazilian waxes. I had a special cream that I smoothed over him afterwards. A shea butter mixed with herbs. It stinks to Jupiter but it works. Takes the sting right out." I opened my clutch nonchalantly and applied a layer of lipstick before continuing. "Anyway, he wasn't even sold on the wax, thought it might be weird. I made him a believer. The experience was very intimate. Almost religious, really."

She was eating it up. "I can imagine," she breathed. "Tell me, what's it like to smooth lotion on a backside like that?"

"Oh." I set a hand on her knee and leaned in. "Let me tell you. Tight as a drum."

She sucked in a breath and leaned away, fanning herself with her hand. "Hoo boy. Am I going to have some sweet dreams tonight." She patted at her forehead with her fingertips. "I feel flushed. I really do. Feel me."

Without missing a beat, she grabbed my hand and touched my fingertips to her face. "Yes, you feel warm."

"I feel hot, don't I? Well." She shook her head, let out a long breath, and returned to her mascara. "I'm so glad I ran into you. Wren, right?"

I was famous in my own right! "Correct. Wren Mallory."

She unscrewed the top of her mascara. "And I'm Rubee Adams."

My breath froze in my lungs. "The blogger from Celebrity Burn?" It came out as barely a whisper.

"That's right. I'd shake your hand, but —" She waved the mascara wand in my direction and giggled. "My readers are going to be beside themselves about this little tidbit."

Oh no. No no no. "Uh, Rubee? I sort of told you that story in confidence."

"Hmmm." She stroked the brush up and down her lashes. "No, I don't remember you saying that."

"Okay." I set my hands down on the counter. "But you can't write about that in your blog. You can't. You don't even understand —"

"Oh, honey. I promise I won't use your name." She smiled and capped the tube. "Anyway, I'm going to use the W.C. now. You run off and have a good time. Maybe I'll bump into you later."

She gave me a kiss in the air and then headed for a black door fitted with a gold "W." and "C." I grabbed my clutch and slinked out of the powder room, feeling sicker than when I'd entered.

I walked zombie-like toward the slate patio and straight over to the stone railing. I couldn't see the ocean, but I could hear the waves breaking on the stones below. When I thought about the story I'd told in the powder room and how it would hit the blogosphere, my stomach heaved. I didn't even know why I'd told it, except that I'd been caught up in the moment, and I thought it was harmless fun… I'd betrayed Jax. Right then, I wanted to be anywhere but in my skin.

"Great party, huh?"

I glanced over and saw a petite woman with platinum-blonde hair pulled into a chignon taking a generous gulp from a flute of champagne. She was wearing a light-blue asymmetrical gown that flattered her figure and her defined arms. "Oh my gosh," I gasped. "Greta!"

She smiled politely. "Yes, Greta Applebea. How are you doing?" She extended her hand.

"Greta. It's me." Then, because she was still confused, I added, "Wren."

She frowned as she scanned my face. "Wren? Seriously?" Recognition registered. "Oh my — what are you *doing* here? I didn't even recognize you! Forget the handshake!" She pulled me into a tight embrace. "I haven't seen you in months!"

Greta and I had been friends in LA, where she was an agent trying to make a name for herself. That was the story of LA: everyone was trying to break in. The fact that she was here, at this party, told me that she'd managed to do exactly that.

"It's great to see you," I said.

She stepped back, her eyes wide. "Look at you!" She shook her head. "Everything. The hair, the dress…"

"Do you like it?"

"Like is an understatement." She lowered her voice. "Did you crash the party?"

"No. *No*. I'm here with Jax Cosgrove." I raised my chin. Jax had kissed me earlier. I was his date. Even if it was all an act, it still felt pretty darn cool.

"Shut the front door! I thought you swore off actors after Griff?"

I laughed nervously and glanced around, but it didn't look like anyone was listening in on our conversation. "It's sort of a long story."

She gave me a once-over and finished off her champagne. "I need to know everything," she said. "By the way, you know Griff is here, right? So's Poppy."

I'd expected as much. Still, my stomach nearly fell through the floor. "Where are they?"

She drew closer to my side before looking over her shoulder. "They're right over there, standing by the pool. I was talking to them earlier. Have you met Poppy before?" She rolled her eyes. "Hot mess. I can't tell what kind of drugs she's on, but they're doing a number on her."

I followed her gaze and sure enough, there they were. Griff looked handsome as ever in his tux, his dark blond curls longer than usual. He'd been working out, or else Poppy was so willowy that he only looked more muscular by comparison. She was nearly as tall as him, long-limbed and, well, just gorgeous. I glanced down at my own corseted figure. I doubted Poppy had to wear a corset.

"She looks hungry," Greta mused, never short on snark. "I went over to say hello just a few minutes ago and she was having trouble focusing. Her eyes were all over the place." She gave me a gentle elbow to my confined ribs. "You should go over and say hi. I swear, they'd probably have no idea who you were."

My palms were suddenly sweaty, my already short breaths coming in swift succession. Seeing them together — I had to stop to take inventory of my emotions. Was this rage? Jealousy? My fingernails were digging holes into the palms of my hands. Greta noticed and ran a hand up and down my arm. "Oh, honey. I'm sorry."

"What's the problem?"

Jax appeared to my left, his face darkened by shadow. He gave a nod to Greta. "Hello."

"Hey, Jax. Nice to see you."

I looked back and forth between them. "You two know each other?"

"We've been to a few of the same horrible cocktail parties," Greta explained.

"Hey." He leaned over to whisper in my ear. "I just spoke with Brennan. He practically offered me the role of Ben on the spot. Can you believe it?"

He paused, waiting for my response, but I was watching Griff and Poppy. They appeared to be engaged in an intense discussion. "Uh, Wren? You look like you're about to punch someone." He placed an arm around my waist. "Want to go for a walk?"

"No." I said. "I can barely walk in this dress as it is." People kept stepping on the train. It wasn't very practical.

He followed my gaze. "You knew they were going to be here," he said. "You don't have to talk to them."

I felt a well of emotion bubbling up, threatening to spill over. Maybe the disguise made me feel safe enough to address all of the ugly emotions I'd been trying to suppress for months. Humiliation. Sadness. Betrayal. I may have tried to take the high road, but suddenly I felt good and angry.

I looked over at him then, at the look of concern on his face. "I'm going over there."

Greta set a hand on my arm. "Honey —"

"No." I shook free of both of them. "I don't want to be calmed down."

I didn't know what I was going to do as I marched over in Griff and Poppy's direction. Maybe I'd stop short and take hold of my faculties, or maybe I'd keep going, plow them over with hostile words or my pinched-sausage body. I gripped the length of my gown in both fists. No one was going to stop me by stepping on that fabric. Griff and Poppy were owed a piece of my mind.

Then Poppy shoved Griff. She actually pushed him and he stumbled a few steps backward, knocking a tray of crystal flutes from a server's raised hand. I froze. The sound of the crystal shattering against the slate rippled through the party until it seemed that no one was talking or moving. Except Griff and Poppy, of course.

"No, *you* don't get it!" Poppy was shouting. "You're the one who thought this was a good idea —"

"Pops, come on." Griff glanced around the patio. "Can we talk about this somewhere more private —"

"I'm done taking orders from you!" She thrust his outstretched hand out of the way. "If this isn't for real —"

"Of course it's for real, Pops! What are you — don't!"

I thought Griff's eyes were going to fall out of his head as she calmly removed a ring from her left hand and tossed it over the side of the balcony. "There. That's what I think of you, and of this charade. We're finished."

"Pops, please —"

She halted her movement, coming close to his face to sneer, "Don't you 'Pops' me, Griffin. We're done."

Then, as if the entire scene wasn't dramatic enough, she turned with a flare of her gown and stomped away. Unfortunately, her first step landed her right in the infinity pool.

A collective gasp waved through the guests, and we watched Poppy's brightly colored gown sink to the bottom of the pool. I glanced at Griff through my fingers, stunned by the events that had just transpired. His face was twisted in a rage I'd never seen before, his hands clenched at his side as he watched Poppy drift downward. His focus was intense.

Time passed, and Poppy didn't come up. She seemed to be settled on the bottom of the pool, her gown billowing around her, her hands floating above her head. My gut tightened. I'd been a lifeguard in the summer months during high school. I knew what drowning looked like. It looked like this.

A woman behind me whispered, "Is she okay?"

Someone had to go in.

I didn't bother to kick off my heels before taking a breath and diving in. My gown was heavy and made swimming difficult, and the heels didn't help, but I managed to reach her. Poppy didn't struggle with me as I wrapped my arms around her, and I was afraid she'd lost consciousness. When we broke through the surface of the water, I heard her gasp for air. Thank goodness. She might not have been my favorite person in the world, but I wouldn't have wished drowning on anyone.

I carried her to the shallow end of the pool and set her on the steps. She was sputtering water and gulping air, and her shaking hands reached up toward her face. "Are you okay?" I whispered. "Do you need a doctor?"

Her lips were trembling as she fought to catch her breath. Her face bore a pained expression, and at first I thought that maybe she'd bumped her head in the fall and that's why she hadn't tried to swim out, and maybe I shouldn't wait for her response before calling for a doctor. Then she grabbed me by my necklace and pulled me closer, sputtering water from her lips as she hissed, "You should've let me drown."

I drew back from her, and she covered her face with her hands. A glance around told me that everyone was watching. When I rose to my feet, I realized I'd lost one of my shoes. I reached down and removed the other one. What was the point?

Then I remembered my hair. My brown hair fell limply to my shoulders, the soft curls gone. My makeup was probably streaking down my face, and my false eyelashes were no doubt on their way to the skimmer.

I looked up and my gaze met Jax's shocked eyes. It was bad. I just knew from looking at him that it was very, very bad. So I did the only sensible thing I could think of.

I ran like hell.

I flew across the patio, struggling against my soaked dress. I flung the train over one arm. It must have weighed ten pounds. All I could think was that if someone stopped me, I'd be tossed out on my ear. Or worse. Fortunately, despite taking an obvious interest in the soaking wet woman running through the halls, none of the guests appeared to take an interest in actually stopping me.

I slipped on the parquet floor, but didn't fall. A quick sprint to the front entrance and a near-tumble down the stone steps, and I had reached the front lawn. My lungs were burning, my feet were already scuffed from the run, and I cursed my luck. Here I was, Cinderella, and my gorgeous gown had turned to rags. I was confident I'd never find the right limo driver, and even if I did, it's not like I could ask him to take me home. He wasn't *my* driver. No, the reality was that I was going to have to walk back into town barefoot, or hope that some kind soul pulled over to the side of the road and asked me if I needed a ride. Then I'd be lucky if I didn't end up in a shallow grave.

The driveway was a million miles long and covered in those little white rocks that are absolute murder on bare feet. It was also edged in thick rows of shrubbery, or else I would've run on the grass. Needless to say, I was in tears by the time I reached the iron gates. Which were closed. Of course they were.

"God *dammit!*" I pounded on the bars with one fist. I pushed on the intercom button and screamed, "Let me out!"

The intercom buzzed back and a calm male voice asked me in an English accent, "Can I help you?"

"Yes, goddammit. You can open this gate!"

A pause. "Are you a guest of Mr. Brennan's?"

How to answer that one? I skirted the question. "I'm trying to *leave.* I want you to let me out or else I'm going to do something drastic."

"Are you now?" There was a touch of amusement in his voice that I didn't appreciate at all. "What sort of drastic thing are you going to do?"

He had me there. I grabbed a hold of the gate and tugged at it, screaming. The voice came back on and said, "That's no good. It's motorized."

I glanced up at the lamppost and saw a black orb beneath. A camera. Fantastic. I was feeling very sorry for myself when I heard the crunch of rock behind me and saw a headlight slice the darkness. I stepped to the side, oddly triumphant. The jerk manning the front gate would have no choice but to open it now, and I'd slide through, right behind the limousine.

Sure enough, the massive gates swung open to allow the vehicle passage. I stepped out from the darkness as it passed. The limousine stopped halfway through the gate and a window rolled down. A woman peered at me through the darkness. "Do you need a ride?"

Poppy. I swallowed and said, weakly, "Yes."

"Come on."

I opened the door, hesitating. "I'm soaking wet."

She kept her profile to me. "Yeah? Me too."

I took that as permission and climbed inside. I selected the seat closest to the door. "Thanks."

She didn't respond. The limo lurched forward and out of the gate, taking a right. I reached up then and felt my hair. It was ruined now, as were my gown and shoes. Would Jax make me pay for them? Then, with a shift of my heart, I remembered the earrings. Fortunately, they were still on my earlobes. I removed them and tucked them into my clutch. Those were safe at least. I was just adding up the rest of the damage when Poppy said, "Who are you?"

Maybe it was too dark for her to recognize me, and of course she wouldn't have expected Griff's plain Jane ex-girlfriend to be at such a posh gathering. "Wren," I murmured. "Mallory."

She was staring directly at me then, her eyes hard and inscrutable. "Why did you run?"

I avoided her eyes. My feet were bleeding. My clever ploy with Jax had gone all pear-shaped and landed me in a limousine with the woman I'd blamed for stealing my boyfriend. A reality star, no less. I started laughing, which only made Poppy glare harder and say, "What's so funny?"

I shook my head, the tears streaming down my face. I was feeling full — of humiliation, of relief that I wouldn't have to walk home, of hope that Jax would get that damn role so I could return to my normal, quiet life again.

I reached up to swipe at the tears. My face was greasy from the thick layer of makeup that Lou had applied to hide my freckles. "I'm not laughing at you. I'm laughing because I think I may have just hit rock bottom."

She watched me, sizing me up. She didn't smile when she said, "Me too." She paused. "What are you going to do about it?"

I set my head back against the seat. "I don't know," I confessed. "Claw my way back up, I guess. How about you?"

The streetlights faded in and out of the vehicle cabin, and as they faded in, I caught Poppy clenching her jaw. "I'm going to settle some scores."

That didn't sound like good news for Griff. But honestly, I didn't care what happened to Griff anymore. It all seemed so ridiculous.

The limo pulled into the drive leading to Breaker House, an upscale inn at the edge of Archer Cove. Instead of heading toward the main inn, it took a right toward the Cottage: a luxurious two-story saltbox Cape with gray shingles and blossoming blue and white hydrangeas in the front. The walkway was made of crushed seashells, which were illuminated by the sconces on either side of the bright blue door. It rolled to a stop.

"Here we are," Poppy announced and gestured for me to open the door. "End of the line."

I glanced from her to the door and back again. "But I'm not staying —"

"End of the line."

Her eyes were hard. I released a breath and scooted across the seat to open the door. Then I stood there, my bare feet on the sharp crushed seashells, and waited, holding the door, while Poppy had some conversation with the limo driver. I hoped she was instructing him to take me home, because being dropped off at Breaker House did me no good. Finally, Poppy exited the limo, long legs first. Without another word, she shut the door and it started to pull away.

"Hey!" I said it, but I was in no real position to protest. She'd offered me a ride — to her hotel. It was like I'd accepted an offer without reading the fine print.

She flung the end of her silk scarf over one shoulder. "The polite thing to say is 'thank you for the ride.'"

The seashells crunched beneath her feet as she walked the few steps toward the front door to the cottage. There was probably someone on duty at the front desk at the inn. I could ask them to call a cab, maybe ask for a towel —

"Are you coming in?" Poppy was standing in the doorway, peeking back at me from over her shoulder.

I balled the train of my gown, squeezing out a few streaks of water. Had I missed a conversation where we'd agreed to hang out for a while? "What if Griff —"

She laughed mirthlessly. "Griff isn't coming here tonight. Believe me." She turned so that her figure was silhouetted by the light in the foyer. "So, what is it? I'm having a cocktail, are you coming in?"

I didn't exactly want to stand out there on those sharp shells any longer. "Sure," I said. "Why not?"

CHAPTER SIX

THE SALTBOX CAPE Cod was only quaint on the outside. I walked into a two-story foyer illuminated by a wrought-iron chandelier lit with lights inside mason jars. Rather than containing the sensible Shaker furniture I'd anticipated, the cottage was fully modernized with the conveniences the wealthy demanded from their version of charming. In the kitchen were soapstone counters, stainless-steel appliances, and a backsplash of sea glass tile. Dark brown leather couches faced a great stone fireplace in a formal sitting area. Poppy flipped a switch, and a fire appeared.

She tossed her high heels into a corner. "I'm going to get out of these clothes. I'm freezing." Then, as if suddenly remembering that I was there, she waved in my direction and said, "Sit anywhere, I don't care." I think it was supposed to make me feel more welcome.

As she trudged up a winding staircase, I considered plopping myself down on a leather recliner, but settled for standing in front of the fire to dry off. The flames didn't seem to give off any heat, though, and I was marveling at how that could even be possible when Poppy reentered the space, this time dressed in black leggings and a beige tunic top. She tossed a large white hotel-issued towel in my direction. "Here. You can dry off."

"Thanks." I wrapped it around myself, still hovering in front of the fire.

"I'd offer you something to wear, but I don't think I have anything that would fit you." Before I could decide what she meant by that, she bounced into the kitchen and called back, "What can I get you?"

"To drink?"

"Whatever. I think we have some munchies."

The kitchen was endowed with an impressive amount of storage, considering this was a vacation cottage. Poppy reached her arm deep into a pantry. "We have some green olives and a can of soup. I wouldn't eat the soup, though. I don't think that's ours."

"That's okay." I sat on a bar stool at the breakfast bar. "You don't have to feed me."

"What kind of hostess would I be? We must have something." She continued to the refrigerator, opening the door to peer inside. "Vanilla soy milk. It's Griff's, but who cares, right?" She set it on the counter. "He's drinking these whey protein shakes twice a day. Then of course he's in the bathroom for hours."

I tightened the towel around my shoulders. "Oh."

She straightened. "He has these chocolate laxatives, but I don't know if they're any good."

"Probably not."

"No, probably not." She shut the refrigerator door. "I need a drink."

Poppy and Griff may not have had much food in the cottage, but they had a bar that was fully stocked with top-shelf liquor. She grabbed a glass and a bottle of vodka, poured a generous serving, and took a big gulp. Then she set the glass back down again and said, "That reminds me, I need to text Griff."

She left the room and returned moments later with her cell phone. "I'm so done. So over it, you have no idea." She paused and glanced at me. "Well, I guess you do."

I swallowed. "You recognized me?"

"Uh, yeah. Griff just about dropped his shrimp cocktail when he saw you making out with Jax Cosgrove. I put two and two together." She took another sip of the vodka. "So you two are an item, I take it? I thought Griff said you were a writer."

"I am."

"Huh. No offense, but you don't seem like Jax's type. The local barista." She stared at the phone screen as if she was having trouble focusing. "Hold on, I have to tell Griff to sleep somewhere else tonight." I waited patiently while her fingers flew across the screen. "Damn auto-correct! It's not 'ducking.'" She held up the phone, the better to scold it. "It's *not* 'ducking.'"

I bit my lower lip. I glanced around the kitchen, looking for a landline I could use to call a cab. Or anyone who would get me out of there. Anyone at all. "I should probably go." I slid off the stool.

She looked up at me in alarm. "No, you don't have to —"

"I'm all wet and my feet are bare." And, I noticed as I glanced downward, bleeding on the tile. "It's okay. I'll just go over to the inn and see if someone will let me use the phone there."

Poppy stared at me, frozen for a moment, and then her face crumpled like a tissue. "You're going to leave me here alone?"

I shivered from the strangeness of it, not from the cold. "Is something wrong?"

She burst into tears, setting her head down on the sleek black surface of the bar and heaving uncontrollably. I'm not certain how long I stood there, wrapped in my towel with my feet bare, watching my ex-boyfriend's newly ex-fiancée crying into her vanilla-flavored vodka. It was a while, but eventually I summoned the courage to approach her and to pat her stiffly on the back. "It's going to be all right," I said mechanically. Really, how did I know that? But what else does one do in that situation, other than to feebly offer reassurance?

She righted herself partially and wiped her fingers down her cheeks. Her mascara was running. "I don't have anyone."

I hesitated. "You have Griff. If you want. I think." From what I could tell, the breakup had been pretty one-sided.

Poppy's chin bobbed sadly as she began to cry again. "He doesn't love me anymore. It's been over for a long time." She grabbed at a dishtowel on a rack at the bar and swept it under her nose. "I was unfaithful. It was a mistake, and I was honest about it, but he won't let it go. He's always reminding me. And then tonight I caught him looking at all of these other women. And you." She paused to cry for a bit and blow her nose into the towel. "It's over. He says I drink too much, and maybe I do. But he makes me crazy. We're toxic together."

She picked up the glass again, emptied it, and tossed it into the sink. It shattered. "Oh no!" A fresh round of sobbing began. "I can't do anything right."

I let the towel around me drop to the floor and stepped closer to wrap Poppy in a hug. In a way, it felt like throwing my arms around a panther. We were supposed to be natural enemies, though I guess we were united as Griff's exes. It was a sisterhood of sorts. "Poppy, you sound like you need some space from Griff." I shifted my gaze to the slew of half-empty bottles. "You almost drowned tonight. Maybe you should consider getting some help."

She rattled as a sigh passed through her. "I'm supposed to start filming next week. Hodges would kill me. That's who it was, you know. The affair, I mean."

My jaw dropped. "You slept with Hodges Brennan?"

"It's sort of a long story," she said. "He promised me the lead in this movie, and instead I got this crummy little sidekick role. And you know who my love interest is? *Griff.*" She balled the dishtowel in her hand. "I want to vomit just thinking about it. Do you have any idea how *humiliating* that is? I slept with Hodges. I ruined my relationship, all for this awful part. And now I have to face Griff on set and it's going to be horrible."

I patted her arm and tried to allow it all to settle in. I've always believed in karma, or some kind of cosmic justice, but…wow. There was no time or reason for me to be smug about Griff and Poppy's relationship woes, however. Not when it was almost midnight and I was standing in their rented cottage, miles from home, in a ruined gown and bare feet. "You sound like you could use some time away. You know, a fresh start."

Her muscles stiffened under my hand. "Oh my God. Yes. You're absolutely right." As she straightened, a smile started to spread across her lips, slow as molasses. It frankly scared the crap out of me. "You're right. I need a break. Thanks, coffee girl." She tossed the bar towel against the counter.

I winced. "My name is Wren."

"Whatever."

She was out of the kitchen, cell phone in hand. "This is Poppy. I need a driver."

I scampered behind her. "What about me?"

But she answered by holding up one finger. "Uh huh. Fifteen minutes? Great." She disconnected the call. "I

119

need to pack." She said it more to herself than to me and headed up the stairs again. Feeling desperate, I followed behind her.

"Wait, where are you going?" More importantly, who was going to be driving me home?

"I'm taking a break," she said breezily. "I deserve it. There's a facility up in Maine, right on the coast. Spa, yoga. I think they have meetings, too." We had wandered into an enormous master bedroom decorated all in white. "I'm going to get refreshed, and I'm going to get sober. Then, I'm going to come back better than ever."

She pulled a large designer suitcase from the closet and tossed it carelessly on the bed. Then she opened a massive wardrobe and reached inside. "What about filming?" I asked.

"You know what? I'm not going to show up." She grabbed an armful of clothes, still on their hangers, and set them into the suitcase. "I'm not. I'm not going to tell them, either. I'm not saying anything. I've been so nice, Red. So patient." She stopped to shake her head at me. "People take advantage of that. Remember this, all of this. Don't make the same mistakes I've made."

She emptied the wardrobe quickly and zipped up her suitcase. "Oh, shoes," she mumbled. "I can't forget those." She opened a closet and stood looking at the rows of shoes inside before saying, "You know what? I'm going to travel light. That's it. We've paid for this cottage through the next three and a half weeks, anyway."

I watched, dumbfounded, as Poppy grabbed a couple pairs of shoes and tossed them unceremoniously into a large designer bag. She then brushed off her hands and turned to me with a broad grin. "There. All set."

"I don't understand. What if there's not room for you?"

"Oh, Red. There's always room when you're paying in cash." She hauled the suitcase off the bed. It hit the floor with a heavy thud. "I wish I could see the look on Hodges's face when he realizes I've stood him up." She lifted her shoulders upward and relaxed them again. "And poor Griff. Hope his part doesn't get cut completely. Wouldn't that be awful?"

She gripped the suitcase with both hands, tugging it behind her across the thick white carpet. "Hodges won't be able to find a substitute in time, that's for sure. Not when filming begins in a week."

She chuckled quietly as she walked past me with her enormous bag. When I saw her struggling down the stairs, I went over to offer a hand. "Hey, thanks, Red."

"No problem." The bag must have weighed a hundred pounds. "I think it's great that you're planning this getaway, Poppy."

"Me too."

"But do you worry about breaching your contract if you don't appear on the set?"

"Not really. Hodges isn't going to sue me. I've got the goods on him, if you know what I mean." She winked.

"No, I'm leaving a little puzzle for him to figure out, that's all."

When we reached the foyer, Poppy opened the front door and peeked through. "Ah! The car is here already. Now that's service."

As we stepped outside, I was surprised to see a black sedan waiting. "No limo?"

A driver hurried out of the car and set the bag in the trunk. "There are people you call when you want to be seen, and people you call when you have to leave in the middle of the night." She waited while the driver opened her door before turning to me. "You need a lift home?"

Relief hit me like a rainstorm. "Yes. I do."

The drive wasn't long, maybe a few miles, but I couldn't have done it barefoot. We didn't talk on the way there — Poppy appeared to be sending some messages on her phone. When the car finally pulled up in front of my building, I could have wept with relief.

"Thanks for the ride, Poppy. And good luck. I hope you enjoy your stay at the spa."

"Thanks. Oh." She grabbed my wrist just as I was stepping out of the car. "I think it goes without saying that everything that happened tonight needs to stay between us. Got it?"

I nodded enthusiastically. There was no way I wanted to be anywhere near the mess Poppy was making. "Got it. No problem at all."

"I'm serious." The change in her voice sent a chill down my spine. "If anyone finds out where I am, I will do everything I can to ruin you. Or your family."

My jaw dropped and I waited for her to tell me she was only kidding. She didn't. "Fine. I told you, this is going to stay between us."

"It's nothing personal." She released my wrist and sat back in her seat, crossing her long legs. "I'm sure you understand."

The driver shut the door and hurried around to his side. I stood there watching as the sedan backed away and sped off into the darkness, thinking that I didn't understand at all. This is one business that I would never, ever understand.

CHAPTER SEVEN

I FLUNG THE gown, the corset, and the shoes into the bathtub and scrubbed my face raw trying to get the makeup off. One of the false eyelashes had survived my plunge in the pool, but I forgot about it and accidentally washed it down the drain. Exhausted, I slept late the next morning, lost in a deep, dreamless sleep that wrapped me like silk, and when I woke, I felt like a new person.

No more games or celebrities. I was going to finish and polish my screenplay, to embrace the new challenge of being ordinary Wren. I was finished playing fake girlfriend to Jax. It was time to move on.

I wasn't sure what to do with the ruined gown. All I had were a few wire hangers, but this wasn't the time to get anxious about something like that. I mean, I'd gone swimming in the gown the night before — was a wire hanger worse? I hung the dress in the closet and set the corset out to dry on a towel rack. Then I showered, dressed, and prepared to start my day.

It was a gorgeous morning, thick with the smells of summer: cut grass and hot pavement, popcorn from a cart by the beach. The whole time I was walking around, enjoying my day, I was thinking about how I'd have to call Jax. The charade, playing his girlfriend — it was fun and all, but it had to end. I wasn't cut out for caviar and diamond chandelier earrings. No sir, no more vain actors for me. As I swung into Hedda's, I felt at peace.

"'Morning, Jess," I said as I headed past the register.

She was preparing and wrapping pre-made sandwiches for the grab-and-go cooler. "Hey. I thought this was your day off?"

"'Tis. I thought I'd stop by and pick up a few items." I paused in front of the display case and greeted the college student running the coffee machine. "Hi, Emily. How are you?"

"Great, thanks." Emily, who looked like a porcelain doll with her light-brown hair and her slightly upturned little nose, was wiping down the counters. "Hey, you missed all the chatter this morning. Rumor has it there was some disturbance on the beach."

"Really?" I looked to Jessie for confirmation. She nodded. "What happened?"

"We're only getting gossip at this point." Jessie set a turkey sandwich covered in plastic wrap on top of a stack and went to work on the next one. "Someone knows someone else who was talking to someone who saw the police cars on their walk this morning."

"Maybe one of those parties got out of control," Emily said. She was pre-med, very studious, and probably thought most parties were out of control. "I dated a guy who lived on the cliffs, and it was constant at night. Drinking and bonfires. I don't think fights were unusual." She paused to brush a few stray strands of hair out of her face.

"Who knows," Jessie said. "I'm sure we'll hear something about it sooner or later."

I studied the decadent goodies in the pastry display: chocolate chip, orange, and lemon poppy seed scones; blueberry, cranberry, and coffee cake muffins; cinnamon rolls; and buns drizzled with glaze. Jessie was adding a selection of large cookies. Jax had bought me a new wardrobe. I might as well bring him a little something to say "thank you."

I walked behind the counter and selected a small box, lined it with tissue paper, and started selecting some pastry. Tough choice, but I picked out a few blueberry and coffee cake muffins, two cinnamon rolls, and two giant chocolate chip cookies. Jessie watched me with interest. "I see you've finally decided to do something about that little waistline of yours."

"Someone is fixing my bike," I fibbed. "I thought I'd bring him something to thank him." I slid the display shut and set the box on the counter. I should've known Jessie wouldn't let me end the matter so easily.

"Him?" Jessie paused mid-sandwich to look at me. "Who's fixing your bike?"

She was watching me, but I avoided eye contact. Was I attracted to Jax? Yes, I couldn't hide that, but the situation was complicated. My stomach burned at the memory of the kiss at the party last night, but see, this was the problem: he was pretending, and I couldn't. My heart was thundering at the thought of seeing him, and my hands were shaking as I closed the lid of the box and taped it shut. There was nothing to do but reclaim control by breaking things off.

"Dennis Callaghan," I muttered, naming the seventy-something owner of Mike's Bikes. Hopefully he wouldn't be coming into Hedda's any time soon. Hopefully Jax hadn't made good on his threat to sell my bike for scrap.

Jessie leaned one hand into the counter and groaned. "You're killing me. I was hoping you were bringing them to some hot mechanic. You know, finally moving on from Griff."

"This has nothing to do with Griff. Who I'm over, by the way." I picked up a piece of a caramel truffle that Jessie had set out for customers to sample. "Anyway, who are you to talk? You're not dating anyone."

"I'm busy," she said, setting one hand on her hip. "I'm starting a catering business, trying to save this bakery, for God's sake."

"Morning, honey," Dad said as he came closer, carrying a silver bowl filled with fruit salad.

"Hi, Dad." I took a small bite of the truffle. "This is amazing, as usual, Jess. Your chocolates are better than sex."

"I'll pretend I didn't hear that," Dad said, not even looking up.

"Yes, plug your ears, Uncle Hank. You too, Emily," Jessie directed. Then she turned to me and lowered her voice. "Don't break my heart, Wren. My truffles are great. I'd even accept that they're the best in the region, but better than sex?" She shook her head sadly. "Then you've been doing it with the wrong people."

I stepped out of the bakery with my box of pastries and headed in the direction of the inn. It was after noon, and surely Jax would be awake by now…right? I paused in front of the police station and pulled out my cell phone. Better call to make sure.

As I dialed, a familiar figure lumbered out of the front doors of the squat, brick building. He was a regular at Hedda's and an old classmate, and I recognized that swagger immediately: Cassius DeLuca. With dark blond hair and a square jaw, Cash could have been typecast as a cop. But things with me and Cash had always been a little strained. I think it went back to high school chemistry, when I'd accidentally set his backpack on fire. I still felt bad about it, even though I'd paid for a new one. Loyal-to-the-end Jessie referred to him secretly as Sergeant Square Pants.

When I saw him exit the station, I turned away a split second too late. "Wren. What are you doing here?"

I smiled tightly and waved my cell phone. "Just making a call."

From the look on his face, that response sounded suspicious. I can only assume that when you're a police detective, everything sounds suspicious. He continued to swagger over to my side. "In front of the police station?"

"Uh huh. Good reception here." I dialed Jax's number and waited for him to pick up, but only got through to voicemail. "Damn," I muttered, and stuck the phone in my bag.

In fairness, Jax couldn't have known I'd be trying to reach him, but being forwarded to voicemail still felt like being stood up. I didn't want to go back to my apartment to wait for him to call me. Maybe I'd go down to the beach, walk along the boardwalk for a while. I gave Cash a friendly wave. "Well, good to see you."

Cash wasn't about to let me go so easily. "Leaving so soon?" He pointed to the box under my arm. "What's in there?"

"Pastries."

"Mind if I see?"

I narrowed my gaze at him, but peeled the tape on the box back and lifted the cover. "See? Just some cookies and muffins."

He actually peered into the box before stepping back with a nod. "Looks good."

I smiled. "Why don't you take one? They're fresh."

"Really?" His face brightened momentarily and he selected a cookie. "Thanks. We've had some excitement this morning. You've probably already heard all about it."

"Yeah, I heard about some party on the cliffs. Archer Cove excitement, not like *real* excitement. Like a body."

A squad car pulled into the lot, but Cash didn't even acknowledge it. He was studying my face. "Have you heard anything about that?"

He wasn't laughing, so I guess it was a serious question. I cleared my throat and resealed the box. "No. I mean, I'm just speculating. Anyway, I'm sure you're busy. I'll get out of your way."

I was walking away when I heard a familiar voice. Then I turned and saw Griff getting out of the squad car.

"Hello, Mr. Dannel." That was Cash speaking, and he had one hand placed on Griff's shoulders. "Come inside. I promise this won't take long."

What the —? Griff looked like he'd been crumpled, straightened, and wrung out. The dark circles under his eyes told me he hadn't slept the night before. I changed direction and walked over to them. They were only about twenty feet away, but he clearly hadn't seen me. "Griff?"

He looked in the wrong direction, then in the right one. "Wren."

And that was it. He froze in place, staring at me and not saying anything. So I came closer. "Jeez. What happened? Is everything okay?" Cash still had one hand on his shoulder, and another officer was flanking his other side. I looked at Cash. "Is he under arrest?"

130

"No," Cash said, but he didn't elaborate.

Griff had changed out of his tux, but his shirt was buttoned improperly. I suppressed the urge to reach out and fix it for him. He stared at me with bloodshot eyes. "Poppy's gone," he said. "I came back early this morning, and —"

Then Griff's face crumpled. Without warning, he reached out and embraced me. "Oh." I wrapped one arm around him, keeping my other on the box of pastries. Then as he started crying, I figured the hell with it and let the box fall to the pavement. "What happened?"

"That's what we're trying to find out," Cash said.

Griff was gripping me tightly, and I sort of felt weird about it, maybe because of the way Cash was eyeing us both. Poppy was at some spa in Maine, and anyway, hadn't Griff dumped me for her? Still, I felt a tug of guilt and patted him on the back. "I'm sure she's okay, Griff. Has she communicated with you at all? Maybe sent you a text message?"

He released me and stepped back. "Yeah. Last night she said she was — wait, I'll get it." He pulled his phone out of his pocket and tapped on the screen. "She wrote, 'I'm ducking out. Don't come back tonight.'" He looked at me with a frown. "Where would she be going at that hour in a town like this? It doesn't make sense."

Damn auto-correct. I licked my lips and avoided his gaze as I thought about it. "Maybe she needed some time alone? Or something?"

He returned the phone to his pocket and whispered, "There's more than that. There was blood on the floor."

I blinked at him, my heart pounding. Blood on the floor? What the heck? Then I remembered the cuts on my feet, and I put my head in my hand. "Oh, Griff. Wow."

I was debating how best to explain the situation. *Here's the thing. I've been playing fake girlfriend to Jax Cosgrove for, oh, about a week now. Funny story. I pulled Poppy out of the pool last night, and she sort of offered me a ride, and she's going to basically ruin me if I tell you this, but —*

"Come on, Mr. Dannel," Cash said, gently taking him by the arm. "Time is critical, and we need to get your statement."

I opened my mouth to protest, but Griff only looked sadly in my direction and said, "Talk to you later, Wren."

Then they walked away, leaving me standing there with my mouth open. I somehow managed to pick up my box. I walked it through the parking lot to the edge of the municipal complex and found a bench. Then I sat down, willing my legs to stop shaking.

This could be fixed, I reasoned. Things would sort themselves out, and I wouldn't need to get involved. This was between Poppy and the rest of the world. Had I told her to vanish? No, I hadn't. They'd find her. It would be fine.

I decided to scrap the walk along the beach. I couldn't get back to my apartment fast enough, to put as much distance as possible between myself and the situation. I locked the door behind me and stood in the hall, biting my nails. Then I did the only rational thing: I headed for the refrigerator, where I'd stashed a box of Jessie's experimental dark chocolate truffles. Some of the flavors were exotic — things like rosemary mint and lemon lavender — but I didn't care. I didn't even bother sitting at the table, and instead ate them all while standing at the kitchen counter. Then I threw the box away. I didn't feel better. If anything, I only felt more disgusted with myself.

I flicked on the television, then turned it off again. I had to talk to someone who would understand. I pulled out my cell phone and dialed my partner in crime. This time, he answered. "Hello, gorgeous," he crooned in a sleepy voice. "I was just getting up."

"Jax. We need to talk."

"We need to do more than that, baby doll."

"I'm serious." A note of panic crept into my voice. "It's about last night. Poppy is missing, and I think I could be a suspect."

I heard a shuffle on his end of the line, and when he spoke again, his voice was calm, but awake. "I'll meet you by the pier. Give me forty-five minutes."

CHAPTER EIGHT

HE WAS ON the beach when I arrived, sitting by himself on a bench a ways from the main stretch. I thought back to that first night when we'd met, when he'd looked like a movie star. Now, he was wearing cargo pants, a gray hooded sweatshirt, a baseball cap, and sunglasses. I could have easily passed him by without a second glance.

I'd bought a bag of popcorn from a stand — ostensibly for authenticity, but mainly because I hadn't eaten anything since polishing off those truffles. I was famished, but I wasn't exactly craving a kale salad.

"Hey there." I slid into the seat beside him, keeping my eyes focused on the sea. A few seagulls were marching around us, picking up trash from the beach and dropping it again. They came running when I tossed a few pieces of popcorn.

He looked in the opposite direction. It was really a bit on the dramatic side, to be honest. "Do you think it's safe to talk?" he said.

"Sure. I don't think this bench is bugged."

He flung his arm casually between us and leaned in. "I've been doing some thinking."

"I thought I smelled smoke."

His mouth tightened into a line. "That's hilarious, Wren. You know, someone is dead here."

"Missing, not dead. And I had nothing to do with it." I looked at him. "But I'm sorry. You're right. I'll show some more respect." I held the bag of popcorn out to him. "Do you want some?"

"I thought you were worried about fat ankles?"

I shook the bag. "I don't really care about that right now."

"You're looking too thin, anyway." He hesitated only a moment before reaching over and taking a small handful. "You should talk to the police. I'm sure it's all a misunderstanding." He popped a few pieces of popcorn in his mouth. "What the hell happened after that party?"

I took a breath. "Look, here's the thing. Poppy gave me a ride back to Breaker House, and she was a mess, Jax. We talked for a while and then all of a sudden, she decides she's going to go to some spa in Maine, which I think is code for rehab."

"Seriously?" He relaxed his posture. "Then that's fine. Just tell the police that she's in rehab."

"Yeah, except she's doing this as some kind of weird revenge against Griff and Hodges Brennan." When I noticed the confusion on Jax's face, I shook my head and added, "Don't get me started. It's complicated, and the short answer is that she made me swear to secrecy."

"Or else what?"

"Or else she's going to create big problems for me."

Jax chuckled softly. "Poppy? She's full of hot air. What's she going to do to you?"

"She said she'd ruin me and the bakery. Not like it matters." Hot tears spilled onto my cheeks. "My dad has to sell Hedda's. It's bleeding money."

I swept at my eyes with the back of my sleeves, weeping quietly to myself. Then I felt Jax's strong arm wrap around my shoulders and pull me closer to his side. "You know how to solve this, right? You show your face to the world. As my girlfriend. Trust me, the crowds will follow."

It was almost too much for me to take, to be surrounded by his warmth and sympathy and to know that it was all nothing but a performance. "This has all started messing with my head, Jax." My voice cracked. "I think it's better that we part ways. I just got out of a relationship with Griff, and that turned out to be nothing but an illusion. I'm…I'm no good at pretending to love people."

"So you're dumping me," he said wryly and raked his fingers through his hair. "You could let me help, you know. What if I bought the bakery myself?"

"That sounds like charity. I can't ask you to do that." I shoveled more popcorn into my mouth. The emotional eating wasn't helping. I still felt lousy. "Anyway, as far as Poppy goes, I was thinking that I could maybe drop some hints here and there, to nudge the police in the right direction. I know the detective on the case. But then I think, doesn't that sort of violate Poppy's privacy, too? To tell people that she's in rehab? It's not really any of my business."

Jax sat back against the bench and stuffed his hands into his pockets. "Explain everything to the police. I still don't see why we have to break up."

I eyed him sidelong. He stared at the sand, suddenly sullen. "Oh, come on now. I'm only fake dumping you."

"Your name is on a few blogs already, and it's only a matter of time before more pick it up. It's not like you can go back to life as usual."

I tossed a few more pieces of popcorn to the seagulls and turned this over in my mind. "It's not about privacy anymore," I said softly.

He turned to me. "Then what's it about?"

We watched the water together for a few minutes in silence because I didn't know how to answer his question. How was it my fault that I'd developed feelings for the gorgeous man beside me? In that way, I was only like thousands of other women. But I'd entered into a business relationship and I'd gone and started to think of it as more, and that was too embarrassing to admit. I was the actress who'd developed feelings for her costar.

"I'm going to head home," I said. "You take care. It's been nice fake dating you." Jax glanced over at me, and I wondered if he felt the same strange fondness I did. "Should we hug or something?" I asked. "I feel strange walking away."

His brow creased. "We can hug if you want to. Do you want to hug?"

And there it was. Okay, so he didn't feel the same. I got sentimental over nothing at all. "No, that's fine."

He sat up. "We can hug. Come on, give me a hug."

"No, really —"

"Come on."

He wrapped his arms around me before I could protest again, and his sweatshirt covered my mouth. "There." He patted me firmly on the back and stepped away, that cocky grin on his face. "You've just hugged the next Hollywood 'It' Man."

He was so damn smug, but still attractive enough to pull it off. "Whatever, Jax," I groaned. "It's been real."

"You lovebirds finished?"

We both jumped at the voice behind us, turning to see a hugely muscular man watching us, his hands folded across his chest. His biceps were the size of small dogs. This couldn't be a good thing. I looked over to Jax, watching for his response, but he looked concerned, too.

"Sorry," Jax said. "Do I know you?"

"My boss would like a word with you two," the man said in a deep voice that was almost a growl. "Come with me."

138

"I'm not getting in a car." I took a step back. My bag of popcorn fell to the beach.

"Ma'am, this is not a request."

"You leave her alone." Jax rose to his feet and positioned himself between us. "This is a crowded beach, and we don't want any trouble."

The wall of muscle didn't look amused. "No one's going to get hurt. It's just a meeting."

"Then I'll go, but she's going home."

The wall of muscle didn't flinch, and he and Jax were locked into some kind of bizarre standoff, with each of them poised to tackle the other. It may not have been obvious under his sweatshirt, but I'd felt Jax's arms enough to know that they could probably inflict some real damage. Beside me, a seagull was pecking at my popcorn.

I sighed. "Look, can you tell us who your boss is at least? I think it's reasonable that we'd be reluctant to blindly follow you."

The wall of muscle kept his gaze fixed on Jax. "My boss is in the car. If you want to know who he is, you need to come with me."

I started to walk forward, but Jax put out one arm. "No. You stay here. I'll go alone."

"And leave you here with this guy?"

"I can handle him."

"He wants both of you," the man said.

I took Jax's hand. "It's okay. We'll go together."

The man rolled his eyes. "You two are adorable. For the last time, no one's going to hurt you, so move it."

We walked past him, giving ourselves a wide berth, and headed toward the black town car that was waiting. The windows on the vehicle were mirrored, so as we approached, all we could see was the image of our own terrified faces. I reached out and tugged at Jax's sleeve, my heart thundering in my chest. What the hell had I managed to get myself into?

We stopped several paces from the car and waited. Then the window rolled down and a face came into view: a middle-aged man with intensely staring eyes that peeked out from beneath two thick gray eyebrows. My breath locked. *Hodges Brennan.*

"Mr. Cosgrove." He smiled in a way that was not at all nice. "And Ms. Mallory."

I swallowed a lump of fear in my throat and clenched Jax's sleeve tighter. Beside me, he was unmoved. "Mr. Brennan," he said.

Behind us, the wall of muscle grumbled. "Are you happy? Now get in the damn car."

Hodges Brennan parted his lips in something between a smile and a sneer. "I'd do what he says. I've never known him to have a sense of humor about these things, and neither do I."

With a sigh, Jax opened the car door and climbed in. I held my breath and followed.

CHAPTER NINE

HODGES DIDN'T WANT to talk. Every attempt was met with silence, or the raising of his palm. The wall of muscle sat beside him and someone else drove. After a time, the car pulled over to the side of the road, and the wall of muscle left again. Not even ten minutes later, he returned with a very terrified-looking Greta.

She slid into the seat next to me, and I felt her shaking. "What the hell, Hodges?" she snapped. "Is this really how you conduct your business?"

"Hello, Ms. Applebea. It's always lovely to see you."

She gritted her teeth and shook her head at him. "Like the goddamn mafia. Most people use phones these days."

He was sitting very still, dressed in pressed khakis, a white Oxford shirt, and a navy blazer. The ensemble was presumably very expensive, though I'd never had an eye for those things. To me, it was like he'd wandered out of the clubhouse at the country club and had decided to spend the evening forcing people into his car under threat of violence. Though as the car ride continued, I began to relax just a little. He offered us beverages and a packet of trail mix, both of which we refused. Still, it didn't seem like the kind of thing one did before harming someone.

Greta turned to me then, and I noticed that she wasn't wearing a stitch of makeup. Her eyebrows looked thinner than usual. "Hey, honey. How are you doing?" She reached for my hand and gave it a squeeze.

"Okay." My teeth chattered, but the contact helped.

"Don't you worry about Hodges, all right?" She gave him a pointed glare. "He's got a flair for the dramatic, but he's harmless."

Beside me, Jax was stone still, his gaze set on the producer. "Are you going to tell us what this is about?"

Brennan fixed a steady stare at him. "Poppy Hayes is missing. I think you're the one who has the explaining to do, Mr. Cosgrove."

"I had nothing to do with it."

But Brennan wasn't moved. "She vanished after leaving my party last night. She was signed for my next film, as are you, Mr. Cosgrove. Now she's being called a missing person." He scowled. "I take personal offense to having my name dragged into something this distasteful."

Jax held up both of his hands. "We didn't hurt her. We didn't have anything to do with —"

"Then," Brennan continued with a sigh, "I review the surveillance footage and pictures from the party. There was some drama, wasn't there? Poppy falling into the pool, and some mysterious woman jumping in to save her." He directed his stare at me, and a blast of ice ran across my skin. "Then I see this mysterious woman leaving in Poppy's limousine. When I research this woman, I find that I have no idea who she is. I figure she's a local nobody, maybe some actress from the community theater. It doesn't take much digging to find out there's more to the story."

My throat tightened, and my breaths came in shallow gasps. "I can explain —"

"Wren Mallory," he continued, staring at me. "A young woman who's had some small-time acting roles, but has apparently left acting entirely. Griffin Dannel's ex-girlfriend. He dumped you for Poppy, didn't he? How interesting that you found your way into my party on the same night your rival disappeared."

"Wren was my date." Jax wrapped his arm around me protectively. "She had nothing to do with Poppy's disappearance. We can explain everything."

"And," Brennan continued like a steamroller, "while you're explaining, I'd like to know what the media campaign is about. Don't look surprised. I follow these things very closely. It's part of my business. Isn't it funny how you've been spotted all over Archer Cove with a mysterious woman? And today's news is that this mysterious woman saved Poppy's life hours before her disappearance. Wren is a hero." He sneered. "Forgive me for not applauding. I'm more cynical than that. But it seems I'm alone, and that everyone else wants to know more about Wren Mallory."

I was looking down at the floor, feeling like a school kid being taken to task by the principal. Here it was, the day of reckoning, when I got my comeuppance for my various shenanigans. "It was nothing," I whispered. "We just spent some time together."

I dared to look up and saw that Brennan was glaring at me again, so I looked back down at my feet.

Jax wasn't easily intimidated. "Give me a break," he snorted. "If I'm guilty of anything, it's liking publicity. Wren is a victim in all of this." Jax was still leaning forward, still urging Brennan to see how harmless it was supposed to be. "It started as a misunderstanding because some blogger saw Wren leaving my room, and that's kind of a long story."

"We didn't sleep together," I added.

"We didn't," Jax agreed. "Her choice, not mine."

Before I could fully register the comment, Brennan said, "So you decided to continue with the misunderstanding?"

"It was a prank," Jax said. "We were playing with the media. My agent and publicist were giving me hell because I've been portrayed...poorly." He stopped, scratched the side of his neck.

"It's a different woman every night of the week with you," Brennan said, sounding like a stern father.

"Okay. Right." Jax released a breath. "But in fairness, that's not entirely true, either. It's just what they report, the way they report it."

Brennan's lips thinned. "Your publicist is right. You need to repair your image before you kill your career. She promised me you were doing exactly that. That you were in a serious relationship. That you were going to be a little more discreet for once. And you." He looked at Greta. "What's your involvement in this...mess? I have pictures of the three of you talking at the party. Are you Wren's agent?"

Greta had her eyes closed and was rubbing at the tension in her forehead. "Hodges, I swear on the hulk sitting to your right that I had nothing to do with Jax's publicity stunt. Wren's not an actress anymore, otherwise, yeah, I'd sign her in a second." She reached over and clasped my chin. "I mean, look at this face. Those cheekbones!"

Brennan's gaze softened slightly as he turned to me again. "Is this true? You're not an actress?"

"No, sir. I'm just a writer now. I have a screenplay."

I don't know why I added that last part. My reputation was more than a little tarnished with Brennan as it was. I felt pathetic the instant those hopeful words left my mouth. Then I chased them with even more humiliation by adding, "It's really an honor to meet you, sir. I'm a big fan of your work and I, uh, enjoyed your party."

Yeah, that ought to do it. We were on our way to being best friends.

He studied me a good long time before responding. "You seem harmless enough," he finally said. "Though I can't imagine what you were doing getting involved with these two."

I waited for him to say more, but he didn't. "I'm sorry, were you asking me a question?"

Brennan remained still, even as the car twisted and turned down the narrow streets along the coast. "Perhaps. Were you volunteering an answer?" He wrinkled his nose. "Don't bite your nails."

I set my hand back in my lap. "Okay. Well, Greta is my friend. And Jax — like I said, I'm a writer and I have a screenplay." In case he'd missed it the first time. "He said he would help me to sell it. I didn't have anything to do with Poppy's disappearance," I whispered, suddenly feeling like I was in a confessional with a stern priest. "None of this had a thing to do with Poppy."

Brennan released a long breath and then held out a hand to the goon, who gave him a large envelope. He opened the clasp and pulled an eight-by-ten inch photo from inside. "I know that Poppy and Griff had a disagreement before she vanished," he said. "And from what I gather, that disagreement had to do with you, Wren."

He handed the image to me. It was a picture of Griff and Poppy, obviously enlarged. She was glaring at him, and he was staring...I followed his gaze. My heart skipped.

"He's looking at you," Brennan said, and reached into the envelope again to remove several more images. "These were taken at different points of the night, and you see that in all of them, he's staring at you like some lovesick puppy, and Poppy is noticing."

My hands shook. Hell, my bones were shaking. "I don't understand —"

"There's chemistry there," Brennan replied. "Attraction." His lips curled into a mirthless smile. "You and Griffin Dannel would make a handsome couple."

I broke out into a sweat. This conversation had bypassed "awkward" a while back, and now it was getting a little weird. "Funny you should mention that, because our relationship is *so* over —"

Brennan waved me off. "I don't care. All I know is that *this* —" he gestured to the images. "*This* is difficult to capture. Griff and Poppy had a chemistry that was volatile at times. That's why I cast them together. Now, I have an opening." He smiled, looking like some evil elf.

It took a minute for the words to settle. "You want me to be in your film? To take Poppy's place?" My stomach began to heave. "I don't feel comfortable with that. At all."

"You'll be cast," he said. "And you'll help me to capture this magic on film. It's poetic, don't you think? Wren Mallory, the heroine who saved Poppy Hayes from drowning only hours before her disappearance, will step forward to take Poppy's place."

I didn't like the way he was looking at me, and I definitely didn't like that he was telling me what to do. "What if Poppy comes back?"

"I know Poppy all too well." He lifted his chin. "This stunt is planned. She wants to make life difficult for me, but I'm going to show her just how easily she can be replaced." He smiled coldly. "You'll be in my movie, Wren."

"Or else what?"

"I'm a powerful man. I can make stars out of nobodies. I can also ruin careers." He looked at Jax and Greta, then smiled calmly at me. "But let's not talk about threats right now. Let's talk about potential." He leaned forward. "I'll read your screenplay."

"So what? Reading my screenplay means nothing." Lest he think I was that naive. I knew my way around rejection, that was for sure. "I'm not an actress. I don't want to be an actress." And less than an hour ago, Jax and I had agreed that we needed to end our fake relationship. Starring in a movie, thinking about the possibility of having to face Griff again...I felt sick.

"What do you think is fair, Wren?"

The car shuddered right and left as we hit a patch of unpaved road. I had never been so uncomfortable in my life, and my skin was so hot that I was amazed my clothing hadn't yet caught fire.

If I was going to put myself through this hell — and let's be honest, that's what it would be — then something good was going to have to come out of it. Then it dawned on me. All of those professionals on the movie set, working those long days. They would need coffee, wouldn't they? And I was the coffee girl.

"My family has a bakery," I said. "It's well-established in town, and the food is top-notch. I don't care if you pay me at all, but I want you to commit, right now, to giving my family's bakery a contract to cater your movie set. That's all meals, every day. Beverages, too." I sat back in my seat and held my breath.

Hodges laughed. "That's an interesting thought. I'll consider it."

"Please," I said. "I can't appear in your movie unless you agree." This would give Hedda's a financial shot in the arm, which the business desperately needed. I paused. "Unless it doesn't matter to you if I take Poppy's place..."

His mouth tightened into a thin line. Clearly, Hodges was a man used to calling all of the shots, and he didn't like this turn. "Are these —" he indicated to Jax and Greta with a point of his finger, "your friends? Do you realize what could happen to their careers if you walk away? What I will do to them for crossing me?"

Greta shifted in her seat. "Hodges, don't put Wren in that position. I've already told you that I had nothing —"

He held up his hand and she stopped short with a grunt, crossing her arms.

The lump in my throat expanded, and my heart scampered as I questioned whether I was doing the right thing by negotiating at all. I was a nobody, plain and simple. But I knew how to fake it, and at that moment, I was faking the hell out of my confidence. "I realize it, sir. But again, if you want to do this the right way, these are my terms."

The car lurched. I didn't even know where we were by then. Either side of the vehicle was surrounded by trees. I hoped that Hodges had planned some kind of return trip and that he wasn't going to leave us on the side of the road.

He tightened and flexed his fingers on his left hand. Finally, he said, "All right. I'll give the bakery the contract."

A flood of relief rushed through my body, and beside me, Jax and Greta relaxed into their respective seats. I felt great, but the feeling was short-lived. "I have one more condition," Brennan said. "You and Jax are to continue this relationship until filming is complete. It's good publicity."

Jax and I eyed each other, but didn't respond. Something in my stomach sparked. So much for being single again.

The driver brought us back to Fisherman's Wharf and we barely stepped out of the limo before it darted off again. "Damn him," Greta mumbled under her breath. She turned to me. "I guess I have to figure out some union paperwork for you."

Jax rubbed at his forehead. "Bastard," he said. "He shouldn't have dragged you into that."

Greta stepped forward then and gave me a hug. Her wiry arms were strong. "Are you all right?"

"I guess so."

She patted my back. "You call me if you need anything, all right?"

I nodded, and she set off. Jax remained by my side, his hands stuffed into his pockets. "So, looks like I can't break up with you after all," I said.

His face was cast in shadows as he met my eyes. "I'm sorry about all of this. You wanted your privacy, and now look." He shook his head. "I'm damn sorry, Wren. You should never have walked me home from that bar."

His anger touched me, and affection surged within my chest. Then I thought of that kiss, and I wondered if dating Jax meant there would be more of that. This was dangerous for my heart, all right. The only thing to do was to focus on the positive: Hedda's had a major contract. Maybe I wasn't so great at failure, after all.

"We should make the best of this," I said, and slipped my arm into his. "You helped me to save the bakery, and I'm going to need your help on set. Maybe we should consider taking this thing to the next level."

He looked at me. "What's that?"

I smiled. "Want to meet my family?"

CHAPTER TEN

JESSIE SCREAMED AND threw a cornbread muffin at me. Emily clapped her hands over her mouth and dropped into a chair in the corner. Dad made me explain three times who Jax Cosgrove was. Basically, the reaction was about what I'd expected.

"I can't believe you kept this from us!" Jessie shrieked, running her gaze from me to Jax and back again. "How long has this been going on?"

We were standing in the kitchen at Hedda's, surrounded by stainless-steel appliances and the warm scents of tomorrow morning's pastries. "Not long," I said. "About a week and a half now. It's kind of sensitive, with Jax's profession."

"It's nice to finally meet all of you." Jax's smile was sincere.

Dad shook Jax's hand and gave him a pat on the shoulder. "Another actor. Better than the last one, I hope."

A flash of uneasiness crossed Jax's face. Just as quickly as it came, it vanished. "I hope so, sir."

Emily crept forward then and slipped a paper catering menu across the table. "Is it okay to ask you for your autograph, Mr. Cosgrove?"

He spared a devastating smile. "Sure. And please, it's just Jax."

I exhaled for the first time all day. This was okay. Good, even. Jax was acting like a normal guy around my family, and while I felt guilty for lying to them, my heart was in the right place. This was about saving Hedda's, and given the right circumstances, I believed Jessie or my dad would've done the same.

Jessie, especially, was electrified by the news that I was dating a movie star. "You have to tell me your secret," she gushed. "First Griff, and then Jax! And here I was telling you that you'd been sleeping with the wrong men. The guy is sex personified."

I laughed nervously and scratched at the side of my neck. "Yeah. He's great, all right."

She folded her arms and stepped closer, lowering her voice to barely a whisper. "Maybe this is weird, but I need details, okay? You don't need to get gross, but just give me *something*."

I glanced over my shoulder, but fortunately Jax seemed to be engaged in conversation with my dad. "Another time, maybe."

"Sure. No problem." She gripped my elbow. "Oh my gosh. My cousin is dating *Jax Cosgrove*!"

I couldn't dwell on the excitement over the relationship. My strategy was to focus on the catering component. Hodges Brennan may have been a bully, but at least he upheld his end of the deal. We had a catering contract signed before noon on Tuesday and barely a minute to collect ourselves before rolling up our sleeves.

"We're going to need everyone here for the next two weeks," Dad said, referring to the college students who worked at Hedda's in the summer season. "They want more hours? They just got 'em."

The order was impressive. Hedda's would provide breakfast and lunch for the cast and crew, which meant bagels, granola, fruit, sandwiches, salads — pretty much everything we produced. We were going to be working double-time, managing the bakery's current needs and meeting the new ones. Dad had called an emergency staff meeting and we were assembled around the kitchen after closing as if we were preparing for battle.

Dad seemed daunted by the inexplicable good fortune, his hair a little bit out of place, his shoulders a little tenser. "But this is good, right, Dad?" I asked. "This is a good thing?"

I can't explain why I was so desperate for his approval, but really — how long had it been since I'd put a check in the "success" column? And even if this deal with Hodges Brennan was technically a complete mess — a check in the success column for the catering contract, a check in the failure column for having to somehow bluff my way through a few movie scenes — I'd saved the bakery. Maybe.

The question softened Dad's shoulders, and he broke into an easy smile, ruffling my hair and kissing the top of my head. "You did good, kiddo."

"It's an amazing thing," Jessie said. "Overwhelming, sure, but...*wow*."

"One thing," Emily said, raising her hand slightly. "How are we going to deliver all of this food?"

"We'll use the van," Jessie said. "I've been catering small events here and there. I think it should suffice, but we may need to make a couple trips a day."

"I could deliver," Emily said.

"She'd be great," Jessie agreed. "She's helped me a few times. She knows what she's doing. I could always go, too."

"Are you kidding?" Dad was firm. "I need you here, Jessie. Baking."

Jessie nodded. "Okay. Yeah, that makes sense. We'll just send Emily, then, and maybe Rob. To help out with the heavier equipment."

"So we have a plan, and now we have to stick to it," Dad said. "We're going to be running a tight ship for the next couple of weeks. We can't afford to make things more complicated than they need to be."

I glanced at the nodding heads around the room. The discussion was ended.

Despite my lack of skills, I would be expected to help out in the kitchen for the foreseeable future. Dad, Jessie, and I worked late into the night planning the menu: assorted muffins, coffee cakes, and scones, hot stations with scrambled eggs, sausage, and French toast, and cold stations with yogurt, granola, and cereals. I was hungry just thinking about it.

"What do you think, Jess?" I asked as we locked up the bakery and headed out into the evening together. It was well past ten o'clock. "Do you think we'll still have to sell Hedda's?"

She hauled her bag up higher on her shoulder and looked thoughtfully at the sidewalk. "It's hard to say. This should help, at least in the short-term. I worry, though."

"What about?"

"The inevitable. This is huge, don't get me wrong. But things have been sluggish for a while," she said. "Even with this kind of a contract, our margins are thin."

The insight was discouraging. "I was hoping — I mean, I thought with this contract that everything would be different." I couldn't stop the injury from creeping into my voice. I was putting myself out on a limb, and maybe there was no good reason for it.

She reached over to wrap an arm across my shoulders and pull me closer. "Let's take it one step at a time. Whatever happens, we're all going to be okay."

I nodded, deciding that I had no choice but to be an optimist for a change. Besides, the wheels were in motion. It was too late to change course now.

I brewed myself a large pot of coffee and stayed up through the night, writing my screenplay. I felt like a woman possessed as the words flowed through my fingertips, and I was so energized by the experience and the possibility that I didn't even drag my feet the next morning when the alarm went off. I worked another full day and spent the evening writing. Wash, rinse, repeat.

And then something happened.

I went to work at the usual time and didn't notice anything out of the ordinary. The early risers came in for their coffee and toast, and then the tourists and beach crowd lined up. I was foaming lattes like a champ, and I set one on the counter and said, "Dave!"

A middle-aged man in a plaid blue Oxford shirt, open at the collar, stepped up to the counter. "Thanks, Wren." Then he gave me a smile and a wink before heading out the door.

I fumbled the empty paper cup in my hand. He must've heard Jessie or Emily calling me. Big deal. But then I gave a coffee with cream to a woman who asked me where Jax was these days, and prepared a double espresso for a teenage girl who was asking whether Jax was *really* that hot in person. "I mean, is anyone going to publish a picture?" She snapped her gum as she asked.

They kept coming, a whole line of people, and when I looked up late in the morning, the line went out the door. Jessie and Emily were scrambling to keep up with the orders, and we had an actual waiting list for seating. A *waiting list*.

"I don't know how long the wait is going to be," Emily sweetly explained to one patron. "We've actually never had a waiting list before."

Jessie counted out change to a customer. "Thanks so much. Have a great day." She turned to me and said, "Can you ask your dad to run to the bank? We're almost out of singles."

"Are you kidding me?" This had never happened.

"Not kidding." She turned as the next customer approached the register. "Good morning. What can I get for you?"

It was a woman with short curly brown hair and sunglasses on top of her head. She was carrying a paperback. "I'm actually just here for — is that her?" She pointed to me. "Are you Wren?"

"Yes. Can I help you with something?"

"Oh," she beamed. "I can't believe this! We're here on vacation, and I just saw the whole story on the news last night."

"The news?" I stared. "What news?" I hadn't seen any cameras.

"It was on that Hollywood gossip show." She snapped her fingers while she thought. "I forget the name. I almost never watch it, but I flipped on the TV while John was showering. That's my husband. Oh! *Hollywood Daily*, that's right!"

"*Hollywood Daily*?" My knees went soft. "The story hit national news?"

"It did. You're a star, sweetie!" She smiled, her eyes nearly disappearing in her soft cheeks. "And I turned to John and I said, 'Well, I'll be. I've got to find that bakery now!' But I should order something. I'll take a cappuccino," she said to Jessie. "And can you autograph the cup for me?"

I froze. "You want me to autograph the cup?"

She nodded. "Make it out to 'Ginny,' if you could." Ginny giggled and moved to one side to watch me work. "My girlfriends are gonna get such a kick out of this. When's your book coming out?"

"Soon, I hope." I smiled as I set to work, not bothering to correct her. "I'm working on it now."

I signed the cardboard sleeve that wrapped around the cup and handed the cappuccino to Ginny once I was done. She'd no sooner thanked me than Jessie leaned over and said, "Can you sign another one for Bev?"

The next customer wanted my autograph too, and a few asked for pictures. We had so many customers that day, most of whom were there to see Jax Cosgrove's girlfriend, that we kept the bakery open nearly two hours later than usual. Dad followed the last customer to the door, locked it, and then turned to us, dumbfounded. "What just happened?"

"Wren happened." Jessie slumped into a seat at one of the wrought-iron tables. "My whole body aches."

Emily stared vacantly at us from the pie display in the corner, appearing as though she might fall asleep at any moment. "I was going to go out tonight." She yawned. "I think I might cancel."

Dad crossed the room to the register and began counting the till. We'd had to zero it out several times during the day, and he'd made two trips to the bank down the street to get more change. "This is unbelievable," he mused. "This has got to be the single busiest day we've ever had."

I was too tired to gloat, or to do anything other than stifle a yawn and say, "Good."

The best part was that my tip jar had nearly overflowed ten times over that day, so I was able to stop by Sam's on the way home to settle my meager tab. The activity was great, but it wasn't anything I could have anticipated or planned for, and I assumed it was a one-time situation. News of my relationship with Jax had hit the press, and the uptick in business was a minor blip.

But the next day was more of the same, and so was the day after that. If it was possible, it seemed that each day brought us more and more business, more and more tourists stopping in to ask the coffee girl to pose for a picture or give an autograph. A lot of them expressed an interest in my new role in Brennan's movie and wanted to know when it was coming out. Many more asked about my screenplay. As tired as I was, I spent each night locked away in my fishy-smelling apartment, typing furiously on my laptop.

We were running out of the basics, flour and eggs, milk and cheese. Dad doubled the orders and called a few of his friends to ask if they were available to help out. Everyone who walked through the door was willing to buy something. Many of them wanted a coffee.

When I told Jax about it, I was nearly breathless. "We've never seen anything like this here. Ever. It's a small miracle."

He raised his index finger playfully and trailed it along my jawline. "What did I tell you? I have the Midas touch."

"You have something," I admitted, and stepped out of his reach. Touches like that could be dangerous.

Maybe I was getting nervous about my return to Hollywood, or maybe it was a matter of being fed up with the bakery decor. Whatever the reason, in a moment of weakness, I called my mom.

Dad wasn't pleased when she arrived at the bakery ten minutes after closing. It reminded me of some kind of showdown as they stood facing each other: Mom looking chic in her floral print sundress, coolly gripping the straps to her handbag, and Dad in his button-down shirt and jeans, wiping his hands on a towel before slapping it across one shoulder. "Hello, Lil," he said. "What brings you here today?"

Mom set her sunglasses on the top of her head and glanced around the bakery. I'd worried it might have been an explosive moment when Mom stepped onto Dad's turf for the first time in — oh, I don't even know. She'd avoided Hedda's for years now. Her gaze was soft, at least. Almost sympathetic. Then she attempted a smile. "Wren asked me to stop by."

Dad shrugged, but the movement was stiff, a sort of forced nonchalance. "You know you're always welcome. We just closed. What can I get you?"

Jessie and Emily were behind the counter, trying not to look too interested in the exchange. Jessie gave a little wave and said, "Hey, Auntie Lil."

"Hello, Jessie." Mom went over to give her a kiss on the cheek and to run her hand affectionately down her blonde ponytail. "You've straightened your hair. I love it."

"Thanks."

Dad cleared his throat. "If I can get you something…"

"I'm actually not here to eat," Mom said. "I'm here in my official capacity."

She didn't elaborate, and I noticed Dad's confused expression. "I asked her to come here," I explained. "I thought that maybe we could do something new with the bakery. Decorating-wise, I mean."

Wrong thing to say. Dad's face darkened and he turned. "That's a nice idea, Wren, but now isn't a good time."

"Oh, come on, Hank," Mom smiled. "The space is charming, but it needs a few updates. I'm thinking window treatments, maybe new countertops —"

"Now's not the time." Dad lowered his voice even though all of the customers had left. Then he directed his gaze at me. "It's not a good time." He started to walk back to the kitchen.

That was his best disappointed tone, and it had never failed to make me feel like I'd done something wrong. Until that moment. "Dad, hear me out."

He stopped in his tracks and turned around slowly. Encouraged, I stepped forward. "Look around." I gestured to the outdated decor: the tables in need of painting; the sad-looking window treatments, yellow with tiny flowers; and the old advertisements hung on the wall, which had been faded by years of sunlight. "If we want to stay competitive, we have to freshen up a little. With all the business that's been coming through the door, we finally have the ability to do something."

His expression was pained. "I didn't want to have this talk now. Not now." He glanced at Mom, then walked over to the door and turned the lock. "I don't know if Wren told you," Dad finally said, directing his comment to Mom. "We have to sell. I've already started looking for buyers."

"She mentioned that there were problems, yes," Mom replied. "Frankly, I'm here to protect Wren's interest in the bakery. Whether sprucing up saves the business or simply makes it more attractive to a buyer, I don't know." Mom folded her arms across her chest. Classic standoff. "It's not a favor to you. I want her to get every penny that we've invested for her." She lifted her chin. "This may be your business, but it's my concern, too. God knows I started this mess all those years ago."

Dad must've heard the tremor in her voice because I saw his guard lower ever so slightly. "Let's not rehash old arguments."

"We won't. That's not why I'm here." Mom's voice had softened and warmed, like melting butter. "I'm good at these kinds of things."

"Your clients all live on the cliffs. We can't afford silk curtains."

"You'd be surprised. I know how to keep costs reasonable. I know a few people who can do me a favor. Let me do this. Please. For Wren."

She reached over and wrapped an arm around my waist, pulling me tightly to her side. Maybe I was feeling especially vulnerable at the time. God knows real hugs were in short supply in my life. I threw my arms around her in response, inhaling her citrus perfume and pressing my cheek against hers. How did she know that I needed that? "Thanks, Mom," I whispered.

"Love you, sweetie." She pressed her lips to my forehead.

I heard Dad cough softly and looked up to see him shifting his weight from one foot to the other. "What do you have in mind? It can't disrupt the business."

She smiled. "Of course not. I'm thinking new window treatments, for starters. We should freshen up that lettering on the door. New paint." She pursed her lips as she thought. "I'm thinking of a light green, maybe. I'll get some samples."

I glanced at Dad. I could tell from his frown that he was struggling not to appear too eager. "New paint? How's that going to happen when we're open seven days a week?"

"It's going to happen after hours, Hank," Mom said gently.

"I can't supervise painters all night."

"I told you, I'm keeping it inexpensive. I'm going to do the painting myself."

"And I'll help," I said.

"I'll help, too," Emily added. "I enjoy painting."

Dad sighed. "I can't pay you for that."

"I can help, too," Jessie said. She was grinning. "Uncle Hank, this sounds great. We need a boost."

He set his hands on his hips and looked at my mom. "You're sure about this? It's going to be reasonable?"

"Promise."

He sighed and took the towel from his shoulder, wiped his hands, and set it back again. "Fine. Have at it. Just as long as I can continue to run the business."

"Business as usual." Mom reached over and tousled my hair gently. "I'm probably going to head up to the apartment upstairs, too. Unless you've already torn down that awful wood paneling and installed new carpet."

"Nope." Dad stuck his hands in his pockets. "I haven't."

"Why doesn't that surprise me?"

I threw my gaze to Dad, but fortunately, he didn't react to Mom's dig. I wouldn't say that my parents had a terrible relationship as a divorced couple, but they weren't warm and fuzzy, either.

"I actually have a lot of ideas for the upstairs apartment," Jessie said. "I can show you everything that's wrong with it." She looked at Dad. "No offense, Uncle Hank. It's just a little outdated."

"Honey, it was outdated ten years ago," Mom sighed. "I've been dying to take an axe to the countertops."

"And the bathroom vanity!" Jessie giggled. "Oh my gosh, this is going to be the best."

"Is that tile still in the bathroom?" Mom wrinkled her nose. "That tile still haunts me."

"It sure is."

I smiled, remembering the old apartment that was my home for so long, its smells and idiosyncrasies — like the creaking third stair on the staircase, or the dark brown kitchen cabinets with their outdated hardware. I started to laugh, but then stole a glance at Dad, worrying that maybe reminiscing about the apartment my mom had always despised would upset him. To the contrary, he started laughing and joining in.

"Whatever you do, be sure to keep that old stove," he deadpanned.

"Oh no," Mom groaned. "That clunky old thing? Please tell me you don't still have it."

"He does," Jessie said.

"It still works," he said, feigning injury. "And it's a classic."

"Dad's right," I said. "They don't make stoves in olive green anymore."

He laughed and tossed the dishtowel in my direction. "All right, all right. I kept you well fed while we lived there, didn't I? I cooked plenty of good meals in that oven."

I caught the towel and balled it in my hands. "In fairness, frozen dinners should only be cooked in an old oven."

Mom sighed and set her hands on her waist. "What is it they say about the cobbler's kids? They have to wear old shoes? I suppose it's only natural that the baker's kid gets frozen dinners. But let there be no mistake: that stove is coming out." She rubbed her palms together. "This is going to be fun. Right now isn't too early to start, is it?"

Dad rolled his eyes. "I'm guessing it wouldn't stop you if I said yes, would it?"

"Nope." Mom rolled up her sleeves. "Now, where's the key to the apartment? If I'm going to work miracles, I need to see the damage."

CHAPTER ELEVEN

ON FRIDAY, I awoke with bags under my eyes and prayed to the gods of Hollywood that there was makeup to conceal them. Between reading over the screenplay and working into the early morning hours at Hedda's, I'd managed less than three hours of sleep. I wasn't off to a stellar start.

The screenplay itself was solid, at least. I wouldn't have expected less from Hodges Brennan, though it was a departure from his usual action-packed adventures. This was a romantic comedy based on a book I'd never heard of, but would now have to read. It was charming and light, and it was called *The Office of Wayward Problems*. I was cast as Maureen, the best friend of the heroine, played by up-and-comer Hayleigh Burroughs. It was a modest role, and I was required to cover the requisite rom-com best friend bases by being a sympathetic ear, a voice of wisdom and insight, and a comedic foil. All things that I felt certain I was utterly incapable of pretending to do on-screen, but was now contractually obligated to do nonetheless. Jax was playing another supporting role, that of the hero's best friend. Honestly, knowing he was going to be on set was the only thing holding me together.

The studio itself had been newly constructed in the last five years — the result of legislation passed in the state to encourage film development. *Wayward Problems* would be filmed in Studio 12. I helped Emily load the catering van and bummed a ride with her to the studio. It was five thirty in the morning when we pulled the catering van to the designated place. "Who are they?" Emily asked as she parked the van. Three people were lingering outside of the studio entrance.

"Maybe they'll help you?"

But they looked more threatening than helpful as they opened the passenger side door. "Are you Ms. Mallory?" A middle-aged woman with a bold shock of fruit-punch-red hair asked when I stepped out of the van.

"I am."

"Great. We'll take it from here." She signaled to the two men waiting with her and said, "It's her. Let's go."

They went around to the back and opened the van doors. "Wait a minute," I said, feeling my heart flutter in fresh panic. "What's going on?"

"Mr. Brennan's orders, honey," she replied in a raspy voice.

Emily watched helplessly as the men began unloading trays of bagels. "What am I supposed to do?"

"I'm the wrong one to ask." She held out her hand. "Keys?"

Emily's fingers closed reflexively around the key ring. "What for?"

"You don't want us to have to tow it, honey. Trust me."

"Wren!" The voice came from my right and I turned to see Lucian speeding over in a golf cart. "Give her the keys. It's a union thing." He came to a stop beside us. "You need to come with me."

Emily and I exchanged a glance. "It's okay, Em."

She hesitated momentarily before setting the keys in the woman's outstretched palm. "I need to make a run back to the bakery. Where will the van be?"

"What time do you need to leave?"

"Half an hour from now, at the latest."

"We'll find you." With that, she walked straight past me to the back of the van.

I looked at Lucian, who was smiling at me. "Come on, darling," he said, and patted the seat beside him. "She'll be fine. Your chariot has arrived."

I had just enough time to give a little wave to Emily before he sped me an impressive distance from Studio 12. "I had no idea this place was so huge," I said.

"Your trailer is quite small," Lou replied. "But private, at least. Perfect for the magic we're about to perform."

"Magic?" I laughed drily. A flash of anxiety waved through my gut. "Don't you mean 'stunt'?"

He took a sharp turn and stopped suddenly, jerking the little golf cart. "I like my term better. Here's your trailer."

He was right, it was small. At least it looked on the newer side, not like the camping trailers I was imagining. "Wren Mallory" was painted on the door in gold letters, but I didn't feel like a star. I felt like a fraud.

"We have two sets of keys," Lou said, handing me a ring. "I suggest you take one and allow me to keep the other. Mr. Brennan has hired me to manage the riffraff, so to speak. Prevent anyone from invading your privacy."

Lou stepped out of the golf cart and walked to the back to collect a cardboard box. I could only assume it was filled to the brim with makeup and the special effects needed to complete my transformation from coffee girl to starlet.

As I walked up the steps to the trailer, anxiety wound through my gut. My acting experience mostly entailed standing around in a background shot. I wasn't exactly feeling confident about this opportunity.

Lou followed closely behind me, lugging the box. "I had a meeting with Mr. Brennan's assistant last night. She should be by at some point to introduce herself."

I took a shaky breath and nodded weakly. "Great. This is all so…*great*."

Lou chuckled softly. "You're not walking the plank, love. Go ahead, open the door. Nothing in there will bite."

I fit the key into the hole with trembling fingers and the door swung open. Something moved toward us, and I shrieked. Seconds later, Jax emerged from the shadows inside, carrying a cup of coffee. "Dammit, Jax." I leaned against the doorjamb and attempted to breathe. "What are you doing here?"

"Always nice to see you, Wren," he mumbled. He was wearing a dark T-shirt and khakis cut off at the knee, both of which drew attention to his finely sculpted muscles and olive skin. "I enjoy starting my day with melodrama. It's better than espresso."

I stepped through the door on shaky legs and fumbled my way toward a seat. "It's not even six in the morning. I swear you have reality show cameras following me and that this is all some elaborate practical joke."

"I'm not that brilliant, baby doll. Sadly." He took a sip of his coffee. "Lou. Welcome to our love nest."

I groaned into my hand. "Please, let me apologize on behalf of my fake boyfriend, Lou. It's all wishful thinking, I promise."

Jax laughed and wrapped a hand around the back of my neck, massaging gently. "She's always crabby when she's tense. It's why I came here early — to loosen you up."

I should've pushed his hand away and stood up, but it felt so darn *good*. For all of his bragging about his skills in the bedroom, I'd thought he was exaggerating, but I had to hand it to him: Jax had magical fingers. I also had to grudgingly admit that he was right about how tense I was.

Unfazed, Lou set the box on a table and shut the door behind him. "You two are getting into character already. Lovely. I'll give you the grand tour." He waved one arm around the tiny space. The interior looked more like a dressing room, with lighted mirrors, boxes of makeup, and a closet and changing area. "You have a bathroom. And a little kitchenette. If you get tired, there's a couch." He set his hands on his hips. "Take some time to get settled in. Then Mr. Brennan wants you out and about, being visible. We may as well get you ready for the cameras, Wren. There are some reporters on set."

I wasn't filming that day, so I'd selected a V-necked sundress in a bright pink, sandals, and a wide-brimmed sun hat to wear. I waited patiently for Lou to perfect my makeup, trying to ignore all of my doubts. Jax had set his coffee down to massage my shoulders while Lou worked. It may have helped me to forget how nervous I was to be appearing in a film, but only because it triggered an entirely different anxiety about making more appearances as Jax's girlfriend. Damn him and his fingers.

Finally Lou stepped away from the mirror and declared, "Perfect!"

And he was right. There, staring back at me, was a face I barely recognized. I grasped the hem of the dress and fluttered it nervously. "All right. Where do I begin?"

Lou leaned closer until his head was just above my shoulder and said, "Might I suggest craft services?"

I rose from my seat, disappointed that my massage was over. "Are you coming, too?" I said to Jax.

"Thanks, but no thanks."

He made a show of lifting his T-shirt to scratch at the washboard abs below. My eyes widened when I saw them, and then I noticed with horror that Jax had caught me looking, and I wanted to combust. He grinned. "I thought I'd finish my coffee and maybe catch a nap."

No fair. He was going to send me out into the wild all alone? "I thought we were in this together," I said.

"Sort of." He sat back on the couch and kicked up his feet. "But it's an ungodly hour, and I woke up early to surprise you, so…"

"Fine. Suit yourself." I turned to Lou. "It's you and me, then."

We made our way back to the area where we'd begun. Lou led me through a back door and down a series of empty halls until we came to a giant warehouse of a room. If I looked up, all I saw were bright lights and wires, but pressed to one side of the chamber was a long line of tables set with the food I'd just delivered. "The spread looks great," I said, as much to myself as to Lou. I made a note to tell Jessie and Dad.

"Help yourself to some food, mingle around a bit." Lou's hands fluttered as he spoke. "Make yourself known."

Lou walked away and I stood still for a moment, deciding where to begin with the buffet. Coffee seemed like as good a place as any. I poured myself a cardboard cup and took a sip. Delicious.

"Hey, are you Wren?"

I immediately recognized the woman who asked as Hayleigh Burroughs, the romantic lead in the film. She had large blue eyes and light-brown hair streaked with blonde and curled in loose ringlets. Mostly, I recognized her large, wide mouth. When she smiled, I thought with a stab of guilt about that blog dedicated to asking the question what could and could not fit in Hayleigh Burroughs's mouth. "Yes," I said, and thrust my hand forward. "You must be Hayleigh?"

"It's great to meet you!" She eschewed the hand and wrapped me in a tight embrace. "I'm actually a big fan of yours."

I blinked several times. Was she messing with me? "You are?"

"Huge." She beamed, revealing two rows of straight, bleached white teeth. "I've seen, like, everything you've done."

I dropped my gaze away to the floor and raised my coffee to my lips. "Wow. That's really flattering."

It was also quite a feat, considering I'd done practically nothing and had been on film for a grand total of ten seconds. I cleared my throat. "I'm very excited to work with you, Hayleigh."

"Same here. And you don't need to call me by my full name. My friends just call me Leelee."

"Is that so? Leelee. It's cute," I mused. "I'm afraid my name is already short, so I never had a nickname."

Leelee's face drooped sympathetically. "*Pauvre petite Wren,*" she cooed. "I have a friend who's just great at coming up with nicknames. Seriously. I should introduce you two. He'd come up with something like that."

She snapped her fingers close enough to my face that I flinched and laughed nervously into my coffee. "That's great," I said.

Leelee rose up on her toes to glance over my shoulder. "Oh, I see someone I've gotta talk to. Can we talk later? Maybe lunch?"

"Perfect."

I sent her off with a tight smile and a little wave, relieved to be alone again. Still, I felt a little strange standing by myself while people worked around me. Off in the far distance, a work crew was talking in a small circle. One of the members was carrying a clipboard and gesturing to the lights above. It seemed like the perfect opportunity to break the ice and introduce myself. Wren Mallory the actress, I decided, was gracious. I emptied the remains of a silver tray of bagels and loaded it again with assorted pastry. It was a bit awkward to carry it over to the crew, but I hoped my smile would be enough to make up for that.

The man with the clipboard was flipping through pages and pointing to the five men gathered around him. "Dave, the lights on the elevator aren't working. Johnny says they're flickering. Can you take care of that?"

"You got it," one of the men said.

The man with the clipboard yanked a pencil from behind his ear, made a mark on the clipboard page, and returned the pencil to its spot. "Good. Joe, I've got —"

He saw me and stopped, bringing the conversation to a screeching halt. "Good morning," I beamed as I presented the tray. "Would any of you like some muffins?"

The six of them eyed me, jaws slack and distrust in their eyes. The silence dragged on, and I imagined tumbleweed rolling between us. The guy with the clipboard turned to his crew. "You guys want some muffins?" They responded with murmurs and shakes of the head and the man with the clipboard shrugged, bemused. "Thanks anyway, sweetheart, but we're kind of busy."

My cheeks were scorching, but I locked my smile in place and responded brightly, "Everything's over there if you change your mind." But they'd already resumed their meeting.

I walked around the set, too mortified to simply turn around and return the tray to the table. Instead, I held the tray up high, a smile tacked onto my face. Every now and then, someone would stop me and take a muffin, utter a quick "thanks" if I was lucky, and continue whatever they'd been doing. By the time I'd finally made the rounds and set the food down where it belonged, I was hot-faced and on the verge of tears. I took long paces back out of the studio and into the sunlight, holding the brim of my straw hat down as I walked to the trailer.

Foolish, I scolded myself. What had I been trying to do, charm them? They were working! I was the only one on this set without a real purpose. The shame of the moment seeped into my pores, and when I reached the trailer, I climbed inside and locked the door behind me. Jax had left a note saying that he'd be back later. I told myself it was just as well that I was alone, even though he would have surely known how to make me laugh enough to forget the entire embarrassing incident.

The trailer was boring, so I went for a walk by myself mid-morning. A group of tourists stopped me and asked for my autograph, and I happily obliged. I even posed for pictures. "That's Jax Cosgrove's girlfriend," I heard one woman whisper to the person beside her. I smiled. I may have been a nobody deep down, but it lifted my mood all the same.

I was just returning to my dressing room when a figure stepped out from the side of the trailer. My mouth went dry, and I choked on my own breath. It was Detective Cassius DeLuca, and he looked downright uncomfortable.

"Hey," he said.

I was suddenly aware that my jaw was wide open. I closed it. "Hey."

I probably looked like a trout, but I didn't care. All I could think right then was that Cash DeLuca was standing in front of my trailer, and I was covered in pancake makeup, and my two worlds — one hopelessly imaginary and the other inconveniently real — were colliding.

178

"Wh - what are you doing here?" I stuttered.

"I was looking for you." He set his hands on his waist. "I hear you're an actress now. You were cast in Poppy Hayes's role."

It's not easy to look indifferent when your mouth is bone dry, but I attempted it just the same. "Right place, right time."

I could see by the way he tilted his head that this was the wrong thing to say. I really did need some kind of buzzer in my life to alert me to these things. "She's still missing, and you were the last one to see her. Why didn't you tell me that right away?"

I gave a sigh. "Now, how could I have been the last person to see her, considering I didn't do anything to her?"

Airtight logic, I thought. Solid. But Cash wasn't buying it. "I'd like to ask you a few questions." He reached into his back pocket and retrieved a flip notebook and a pen. "Can you tell me the nature of your relationship with Poppy Hayes?"

"Oh my God, you actually take notes on paper?" I shook my head. "Sorry, I don't see much of that any more. So, uh, me and Poppy?" I looked up at the clouds as I considered the question. "We sort of don't have a relationship? More like, she had a relationship with my ex-boyfriend, and that's pretty much it."

"You never knew each other?"

"Nope."

"But security cameras caught you climbing into her limousine on the night she disappeared." His eyebrow arched victoriously. "Maybe you want to reconsider your answer."

Not really, Sergeant Square Pants. "There's nothing to reconsider. She offered me a ride, that's all. It was the first time we spoke." I paused. "Aside from that time she came into Hedda's with Griff, but we didn't speak then."

"Why would she offer her fiancé's ex-girlfriend a ride in her limousine?"

I shrugged. "Maybe because I'd saved her from drowning in the pool minutes earlier? I don't know. People do weird things." I eased myself down onto the steps of the trailer. "I didn't hurt Poppy, all right? She said she was heading somewhere in Maine but she didn't tell me where."

He froze, his ballpoint pen poised above the paper. "So you know where she is?"

"No. She didn't tell me." I said it slowly, stressing each word. "Some spa. That's all I know, I swear." I made an "X" across my heart for emphasis. "Why are you so convinced that there was, uh, foul play?"

"There are a few details that are troubling, but maybe you can shed some light," he replied, almost with apology. "Bloody footprints on the floor, for one. Broken glass in the sink. Her bag is missing, and so are most of her clothes."

I reached up to rub the tension that was gathering across my forehead. "That blood on the floor was mine. I cut my feet when I ran away from the party. And the broken glass in the sink? Poppy broke it. And like I said, she went to some spa in Maine and packed her own bags."

"What's all this about?" I hadn't heard Jax approach, but he came up between me and Cash now, his face stern. "Is something wrong here?"

Sergeant Square Pants puffed out his chest, but Jax still had several inches on him. "Detective DeLuca with the Archer Cove P.D.," he said. "Just asking a few questions concerning Poppy Hayes's disappearance."

"And I'm sure Ms. Mallory has told you everything she knows," Jax replied. "Is there anything else?"

Cash's gaze jumped from Jax to me and back again. "I think that's all. For now." He folded up his notepad and stuck it into his pocket. "I'd suggest you not leave town, Wren."

Jax crossed his arms with a soft laugh. "Is that really necessary, detective?"

But Cash pretended not to hear him and set off toward the studio. As I watched him walk away, Jax mounted the stairs and reached out a hand. "Come on. He's not worth another second of your time."

I slipped my hand into his and stood. "Thanks. I knew him in high school. He's mostly harmless."

"You must have turned him down for the prom," Jax said with an amused smile. "There's history of some sort there."

I slipped out of my sandals. They may have been beautiful, but they were also cutting off the circulation in my smallest toe. "Not exactly. I sort of set his backpack on fire."

"Oh, of course you did." He sat down on the couch with a laugh. "That was going to be my next guess."

His laugh was infectious, or else I'd been having a really bad day. I climbed into the seat beside him and pulled my legs up. He was so handsome, the way his eyes crinkled when he laughed. I glanced down at the floor. "He still hates me for it. The fire, I mean."

"Nah. I'd say it's the opposite, and he secretly wants you. Don't play shocked with me." He stretched back out on the couch and clasped his hands behind his head. "Just so you know: if you and I had met at a party before I reformed my image, I would've hit it. I'm just saying. You have this smart-girl thing going on. It's kind of hot."

"Wow, Jax. That's a lovely sentiment. Really. You sound like a poet."

"I'm taking a nap." He stretched out on the couch, setting his legs over mine. "But you should know I can last for hours, sweetheart. Meditate on that."

I chuckled and patted him on the knee as I rose to my feet. "Yeah, all right. I think that's a medical condition you're supposed to call a doctor about."

It was all a joke, of course. Nothing more than our usual banter. I'd learned from Griff that there was a lot of sitting and waiting while on set, so I'd printed out my screenplay to edit. "Mind if I work?"

"Nope." He flung an arm across his eyes.

I propped my feet up on the table and leaned back in my chair, pen in hand. The quiet lasted for less than three minutes.

"Hello?" A cheerful woman's voice called out from the trailer door, and seconds later, she pushed her way inside without waiting for an invitation. "Wren! So good to meet you. I'm Cheryl Millhouse, Mr. Brennan's assistant."

Cheryl had a set of perfectly straight, perfectly white teeth and a large smile to go with them. She looked like a local news reporter, with a sharp, no-nonsense chin-length blonde bob and enough makeup to even out her skin tone to perfection. She was wearing a khaki skirt, a blue knit tank, and a matching cardigan that she'd tied around her shoulders. Her pep was contagious, no matter how early it still was.

"Nice to meet you," I said. We shook hands.

She shut the door behind her. "Honestly, I'm impressed by your media blitz, sweetheart. I've never seen anything like it. You're in all the blogs, being picked up by national celebrity news shows. You've got to tell me what kind of photos you have to get that kind of attention."

Her stream of chatter momentarily flustered me. "Sorry?"

"Tell me you have blackmail photos of some kind." She reached forward to touch my arm conspiratorially. "Who did you catch doing what? Because you're suddenly hot, and from what I can gather, no one knows why."

She folded her arms across her chest and waited for my response, which was delayed somewhat as I struggled to figure out what I was being accused of. Fortunately, Jax never seemed at a loss for words. "She's famous because I let her touch me," he yawned.

Cheryl shot him a look that told me she knew better. "Who *don't* you let touch you, Jax? Don't mean to put you on the spot, sweetie. Just know that you have my utmost and sincere admiration for whatever you're pulling off here. I understand when people are famous for a film or a television show, but it's the ones who seem to be famous for nothing at all that fascinate me. Anywho." She pulled a cell phone from her back pocket and started tapping at it with a skinny leopard-print stylus. "I'm not here to chat. I wanted to introduce myself and see if there's anything you need from me."

Five minutes alone seemed like too much to ask today. "Not a thing." I kicked my feet back up on the table.

"Then I'll show myself out," she said with a broad grin. "When you decide to become high maintenance, you let me know."

She shut the door behind her and Jax and I looked at each other. "You look tense," he said. "If you want to shag —"

I groaned. "No. For God's sake."

He leaned back on the couch. "Well, the offer still stands."

CHAPTER TWELVE

JAX HAD TO meet with someone in Wardrobe, but I didn't want to stick around for that. Instead I headed to Studio 12. I was hoping to meet a few of the other actors. There was also the fact that I wasn't actually a jaded starlet, and I was intrigued by the idea of being on a major movie set. I wanted to see how it worked, in a way that brought no attention to myself whatsoever.

All of my scenes were going to be filmed on the office set. It was a gray cubicle jungle, really. When I walked on the set, I immediately saw Hayleigh Burroughs blustering her way through the interview scene. The actor playing her boss looked familiar, but I'd forgotten his name. Someone shouted, "Cut!"

I stood near the back, well behind the cameras and the crew crowded around the actors, and watched breathlessly as the director rose from a box he'd been sitting on and approached the actors. I already knew that his name was Alex Sherapovna. He was dressed in jeans and a brown herringbone jacket and his hair was streaked with gray, but his face appeared younger than his almost fifty years. "Hayleigh, honey. Remember: you need this job because your grandmother is going to be evicted from her house."

The young actress watched him, her blue eyes saucer-like. "Yes." She reached up to scratch at her head. "I'm sorry, but this is driving me crazy."

Alex shouted over his shoulder, "Can we do something about her hair?" He looked back at her. "We need to see some desperation. When he tells you that you're not exactly what they're looking for, we need to *feel* your heart break."

A young woman in dark-rimmed glasses ran up and unfastened whatever pins and barrettes had been holding Hayleigh's hairstyle in place. The actress looked at him, stone-faced, as her hair was fixed. "I just thought that right now, it was more about proving something to herself than saving her grandmother. I thought that she didn't fully appreciate what her grandmother was going through until later on."

Alex crouched down to speak with her. "You're giving me feisty. I don't want feisty. I want vulnerable."

"But feisty is there, right? Rita has this energy, and I want to make sure that it comes through."

"It's coming through," he assured her with a pat on the knee. "But what I need you to do is to show us Rita's underbelly. Show us the softness. Got it?"

She couldn't nod because her hair was being violently tugged into place by the woman with the glasses. "Got it."

"Good."

He turned and pointed to someone behind him. "Joe? We need to fix the lighting."

As I was absorbing the unfolding scene with a sense of wide-eyed wonder, someone came up right beside me and said, "You're Wren Mallory, right?"

I looked and saw a fresh-faced man beaming at me. I smiled back, ever the gracious one. "Yes, I am."

"I'm George. I'm a PA."

I blinked. "PA?" I searched my brain for a moment, then remembered. "Production assistant. Of course. Nice to meet you, George."

"I'm heading over to craft services. Can I get you something? A coffee or water? Something to eat? It's going to be a late night."

I wasn't filming, but I needed to head out soon. I was needed in the bakery. "I'll be fine, thanks."

"You sure?" He pulled out a pen and notepad and was poised to write. "You seem tired. How about a coffee or a tea? It's no trouble."

I considered. "Well, maybe —"

"Is this guy bothering you?"

I jumped, not just at the voice, but at how close it was. *Griff.* I hadn't even heard him approach. He narrowed his eyes at George. "Trying to get a date? Leave her alone, pal."

It was like something out of a bad movie, and I rolled my eyes. "He's fine." I stepped between Griff and George, who was starting to wilt under the scrutiny. "He was offering to get me a coffee, that's all."

"Do you want a coffee?" Griff said. "Because I'll get it for you. You." He turned back to George. "Don't you have something better to do than hassle the talent?"

Hassle the talent? Oh, honestly. "He wasn't doing anything wrong —"

George took a step back and gave me a patient smile. "I'll go. But if you need anything, Ms. Mallory, you let me know."

"I will. Thank you, George." I looked at Griff, who was standing much too close for my comfort. "Do you always boss production assistants around like that?"

"Sorry," he said, without looking it. "I've had a rough few days. I'm not myself." He stuffed his hands into his pockets and shifted from foot to foot. "Do you think I should go apologize to him?"

"Yes. Absolutely I do. He —"

Just then a loud voice boomed, "Quiet on the set!"

Griff reached for my elbow and nodded behind us. "Come on," he whispered. "Let's get out of here." So much for an apology for poor George.

We left the set and stepped outside into the afternoon sunshine. "Funny meeting like this again," he said once the door had closed behind us. "When my agent told me you'd been cast, I thought I'd heard wrong. But here you are." He looked me up and down. "I guess I'm wondering why."

I won't lie — having my ex-boyfriend of two years in front of me again was a little surreal. Watching him puff out his chest to impress me was even weirder. All I saw was the guy who dried his socks over the bathtub and watched late-night television in his boxers with one of those muscle-gaining milkshakes. He would stick his fingers in the peanut butter jar rather than opening a drawer and grabbing a spoon. Sure, he was a star now, but knowing too much about a person makes them less impressive.

I cleared my throat and stuck out my hand. "Nice to see you too."

He wrapped my hand in both of his and gave a gentle squeeze. He also held my gaze in a way that felt, well, creepy. Then I remembered that when we were both wondering why we couldn't break through in the Biz, he'd gone to some seminars on becoming unforgettable. One of the tips was to make eye contact like the other person was one of the most fascinating subjects in the world. The technique made him unforgettable, all right. "You are full of surprises, Wren." His voice was oddly husky. "I had no idea you were still interested in acting."

"Guess the bug bit me." I laughed too loudly. "It's just…I never considered myself an actress, but then there was this opportunity." I paused when I realized that I'd referred to Poppy's disappearance as an opportunity.

"Sorry, that sounded callous, didn't it? How are you holding up?"

"All right, all things considered. Everyone's been supportive, and I've been looking forward to seeing you to formally thank you for...everything."

He released my hand and shoved his hands back into his pockets. He looked down at the ground, imitating the appearance of someone forlorn. At least I think that's what he was going for.

"You don't have anything to thank me for," I said.

He picked up his head to gaze into my eyes, but it was really just staring. Intensely. "You saved Poppy from drowning. It would have been a terrible way to go."

"No problem." I cleared my throat and darted my gaze anywhere but to his face. "Have you heard from Poppy?" I asked, even though I thought I knew the answer.

"Poppy and I were having problems," he confided. "It's been over for a long time."

Once upon a time, Griff and I had been as close as any two people could be. In those days, I might have thought it strange if we'd been in the same room and he hadn't made an effort to stay close by my side. At that moment, when he edged closer, I felt an unexpected revulsion. My personal boundaries had closed me off to Griff. Any bond we'd once shared had vanished.

"She never understood me," he continued. "Not really. We led separate lives for the most part."

I smiled tightly. Politely. "You could've fooled me. You always seemed so close in all of those photos." My voice sounded a little shrill to my ears.

He chuckled softly and bobbed his head. "It's all part of the deal. Smoke and mirrors is what we signed up for, it's what we do for a living. Meanwhile what happens in here —" he jabbed a finger against his sternum. "That's off-limits. To the press, definitely. Sometimes to those closest to us."

I was certain that if I'd caught myself in a mirror at that moment, the look on my face would have been something out of a horror film. Open up a closet and have a werewolf jump out at me, and bam! Same face. Because Griff was being so weirdly horrifying at that moment that I couldn't even pretend that what he was saying made any sense. The worst part was, he was certain that I would agree, like it was part of joining the union that all actors agreed to think of ourselves as chimeras, showing one face for the sake of the cameras, another for those we cared about.

A thought struck me like a blast of ice to the heart: how well had I known Griff, anyway? How much of himself had he kept off-limits? I felt uneasy.

Griff was still talking, still edging closer to my side. "You want to grab something to drink and maybe run some lines? We're shooting a scene together tomorrow."

Yes, we had a few scenes together. He was unfortunately cast as my love interest in a secondary story line. But he was turning my stomach at the moment.

"Maybe another time." I tried to keep my voice syrupy. "I'm sure you've had a long day. You should rest up for tomorrow."

He ran his fingers through his highlighted hair. No, it wasn't the lighting. That hair was definitely ridiculous. "Right. I mean, it's cool. I'm fine, I just." I braced myself as he brought his hand down and looked at me with a gaze that was loaded with meaning. "I just wanted someone to talk to."

No. Just no. Wasn't that how I'd gotten into this mess in the first place, because I apparently attract actors who "just want to talk"? I took a deep breath and held it. Where *was* my fake boyfriend, anyway? Shouldn't he be on the set, fighting to keep his hands off of me?

"Oh, just a sec," I said, pretending my cellphone had just vibrated. "Let me check to make sure…"

I pulled up Jax's number and texted him. `You have to come to the set. Now. Griff is trying to hit on me.` I hit send.

"Is it important?" Griff was still standing too close, trying to read over my shoulder. Had I never noticed that he had no manners at all? What was wrong with me?

"I — I thought it was my doctor." I clung to the phone. "So, yeah, about that scene — ah!" My phone vibrated and I saw a message from Jax. `On set now. Where are you?`

"Oh, looks like Jax is here." I beamed and texted our location. "You two know each other, right?"

"Sure, I know Jax." Griff took a step back. "Are you two still…?"

"Dating?" I shrugged casually. "We're working on things. We'll see what happens." I tucked the cell phone back into my pocket. "Hey, but you know, we should definitely get together tomorrow morning to run our scene. Definitely. Why don't I stop by your trailer around eight?"

"In the morning?" His eyebrows nearly struck a cloud. "You like to get up early, huh? But sure. Stop by then."

"Terrific."

Jax came around the corner, driving a golf cart and carrying a giant bouquet of red and white roses. I gave him a wave and a sugary smile. "Hey, baby. Who are those for?"

He pushed the bouquet gently into my arms. "Hi, sweetheart. I've been trying to reach you."

Maybe I'd had too much sun, or maybe it was the glimpse of the tattoo that wrapped around his upper bicep, but Jax struck me then as a gorgeous knight on his white steed: dashing, powerful, and completely irresistible. Once again, he'd come to my rescue. I reached up to wrap my arms around his shoulders, bouquet of roses and all, and without a thought at all, I pulled him into a kiss. He moaned softly and reached down my back to pull my hips closer to his, dissolving the space between us. He tasted slightly minty, and his lips were soft and warm. Through his chest, I felt his heart thundering. We stayed that way for what felt like hours. Then I heard a shuffle behind us, and Griff clearing his throat.

I stepped away with a soft giggle. "Sorry. It's just that I missed you."

Jax grinned. "That's understandable. It's been about an hour now." He extended his hand to Griff. "Good to see you, man."

"You too," Griff said.

"Come on, baby," Jax said, pulling me by the waist. "Let's grab dinner."

I laughed and waved at Griff with my fingers. "See you tomorrow, Griff."

I climbed into the passenger seat of the cart. Once we were out of earshot, I slumped back against the seat and said, "Your timing was perfect. I think he was hitting on me."

"Can you blame him?" Jax eyed me sidelong. "Is that why you kissed me? To make him jealous?"

When I realized I didn't have an answer to his question, I was embarrassed. What *had* I been thinking? "I — I was just being spontaneous. We're dating, remember?" I deflected the scrutiny with a compliment and smelled the roses. "These were a nice touch."

"Brennan made it clear that I'm to continue to date you. You're the new blog sweetheart, by the way."

"That's nice." I frankly didn't care what the blogs said. I was due back at Hedda's, or else Jessie was going to send a search party. "I'm going to clean up and head back out again. I'm baking tonight."

"I thought we were going to spend more time together?"

"You sound like a real boyfriend." I patted his arm. "I'm on the set all day tomorrow. Can we catch up then? Be spotted having lunch or something?"

"Okay." He sounded disappointed, which was altogether disconcerting to me.

"Sorry, bud, but now we've got this big catering contract and it's all hands on deck." I shifted in my seat to face him as he pulled up the cart in front of the trailer. "My family needs my help."

Jax mulled this over and nodded. "I get it. It's fine. Your family comes first."

We'd arrived at the trailer by then. He waited outside while I changed and scrubbed off my makeup. I set the flowers in a bowl full of water and made a note to bring a vase the next morning. Then Jax drove me to the catering van, where Emily was waiting to drive us back to Archer Cove.

CHAPTER THIRTEEN

THE BAKERY WAS a scene of loosely organized chaos when I arrived. Dad and Emily and I unloaded the van while Jessie managed the kitchen, pulling baking sheets in and out of the ovens and then returning to add ingredients to the mixer. As I watched the scene, it occurred to me that maybe I'd made things worse for them, after all. Maybe in my effort to help the bakery, I'd only managed to make life more difficult. "How's it going?" I ventured to ask when I had a moment alone with my cousin.

"We'll get it done," Jessie said as she cracked eggs into what appeared to be a butter and sugar mixture. "How did the first day go? Were there any problems?"

I leaned back against the counter and fluttered my lips in a sigh. "Gosh, Jess. I don't know how much longer I can keep this up. I don't know whether I'm coming or going, and the sudden spotlight...Do you know that people stopped me for my autograph today? *Me*. A complete nobody."

"Not anymore," she said, and blew a strand of hair out of her eyes. "This rush of business? It's not slowing down. You should've seen the lines today. Lots of the customers were asking where you were, or if you were with Jax." She chuckled. "Your dad had to amend the order for this week. They almost cleaned us out."

"Oh. Wow."

I pushed off the counter and walked mechanically toward the rack where we hung the aprons. Being an overnight celebrity should have been good news, but it left my bones rattling. I wasn't yet sure what any of this would mean, long-term. I had a sudden, overwhelming desire to run back to my apartment, shut the door, and hide under the covers. "Hey, Jess?"

I stopped mid-thought to watch as my dad poured milk into a second mixer and Emily carefully stacked scones onto a tray. Jessie scooped a cup of flour and added it slowly to the mixture, sending puffs of white into the air. They needed my help, and all I wanted to do was leave.

"Hmm?" Jessie raised a rubber spatula and swept it down the side of the bowl.

I stood upright. This was no time to think about the bizarre turn my life had taken. I reached for an apron. "What can I help with?"

She set me to work on scones. Jessie was determined to teach me something about baking, even if Hedda's was

197

possibly short-lived and we were both weeks away from unemployment. I was slicing cold butter into the flour mixture when Dad called out over his shoulder, "Wren? Jax is here."

He'd taken the back way, coming to the screen door in the kitchen. He was wearing a dark cashmere sweater and jeans. Casual, but definitely sexy. He smiled when he saw me. "Hey, Wren."

"Hey." My smile sprouted straight from the warmth spreading through my center. "You — what are you doing here?"

"I wasn't busy tonight." He stepped closer, keeping his gaze fixed on mine, lowering his voice. "I wanted to see you."

There are moments you remember, times when you feel complete. Standing there, facing Jax, being the same as we always were but somehow entirely different — I felt the significance. No snark, no cameras. No reason to think he wasn't sincere. Heat bloomed across my cheeks as I leaned against the doorjamb. "Look. Things here are sort of..." I glanced over my shoulder at the flurry behind me.

Jax followed my gaze. "Busy?"

"Yeah. They need my help. Would you mind —"

"Can I help, too?"

The offer came so quickly and eagerly that I was caught off-guard. "Are you sure?"

Jax inched closer, leaning down slightly. "Let me get this straight. My options are to head home alone or to stay here with you, right?"

His voice was soft and deep, his words meant for my ears only. An electric current bristled across my skin. "Right."

"Then where do I get my apron?"

I grinned. "This way. I hope you like pink ruffles."

I'm certain he could have pulled it off, but I didn't make him wear the ruffles. We found one of my dad's simple black aprons. I have to say, Jax even made that look kind of hot.

"Okay." He rubbed his hands together. "What are we baking?"

Jessie watched us with a sly smile, and I just knew that she was going to give me the third degree the second we were alone. I didn't care. "Tonight, the word is 'scones,'" I said.

We baked scones for hours. Cranberry white chocolate chunk, orange, cinnamon chip, blueberry, and cherry chocolate. We melted butter, measured flour and sugar, and cut triangles of dough, all under Jessie's watchful eye. When the first batch came out of the oven, we sampled it.

"Wren, these are delicious," she gasped.

She sounded so surprised that I knew she was being honest. The thing is, they were. At least, they weren't half bad. "I had some help," I said, and bumped Jax with one hip.

"You told me you couldn't bake," he said through a mouthful of cinnamon chip scone. "You've been holding out on us."

"I followed the recipe." The modesty wasn't false — I was as flummoxed as anyone else by my success. It felt good to be flummoxed in a good kind of way for once.

Jessie took another bite. "Seriously, what's your technique? These are *really* good."

I turned the scone over in my hand and frowned at it, as if I could discern the answer to her question if only I studied it hard enough. "I'm not sure. I just mixed it all up."

Dad took a bite of an orange scone. "Whatever you did, try to keep doing it. These are better than mine."

"You're going to put us out of a job." Jessie chuckled and wiped her fingers on her apron. "All right. Back to work."

As we baked, I was trying to figure out exactly what Jax and I were becoming. All I knew was that he wouldn't stray too far from my side, and my heart was getting a workout having him so close. Even so, by eleven o'clock I could barely keep my eyes open.

I yawned into my elbow. "Are we finished? I have to get home."

Jessie stifled her own yawn. "Yeah, I think we're done. Thanks for your help. You too, Jax."

"Get home," said Dad. "Jessie and I will lock up."

Emily had left earlier, so Jax and I were alone as we stepped outside into the warm summer night. "I'll walk you home," he said.

"You don't have to."

He didn't reply except to take my hand in his. His skin was warm, his hand strong. "Nice night."

"Yes." The word squeezed around the knot in my throat.

Archer Cove was far from city lights. As a result, the sky at night was inky dark but brilliantly lit with stars. I allowed myself to gaze up at them as we walked, lost in the expansive beauty of the display.

Jax broke the silence. "What is it about you, Wren? I've wanted you from the second I saw you sitting at that bar, typing away on your laptop while wearing that ridiculous baseball cap." He stopped in his tracks and pulled me closer, pressing my hand against his heart. "You kissed me this afternoon. I know you weren't acting. You want me, too."

I could barely breathe under the heat of his stare, the weight of my need for him. "Yes," I whispered, terrified at the confession.

The earth shifted below us or we moved closer together, but his lips were pressing against mine, and I was tugging at him, running my hands over his beautiful shoulders and down his arms. I no longer cared if it was only one night and never again. I wanted that one night with Jax Cosgrove.

"Quick," I whispered when I managed to break away from his kiss. "This way."

We took the shortcut, crossing through neighboring yards and cutting across Crabby Andy's back lot. When we reached the steps to my apartment, I was grateful we'd missed the cooks' smoke break. I mounted the stairs and Jax stopped, pressing me against the rail to slide his lips down my neck and his fingers up the back of my shirt. I no longer remembered why I'd resisted his advances. His touch was magic.

I heard a sharp intake of breath and felt the shudder pass through his frame. He pulled me closer and whispered, "This will change everything. Are you sure?"

I set my hand against his cheek to feel the emerging stubble. "I've never been sure of anything in my life until now."

We walked up the steps and I unlocked the door. We never made it past the kitchen.

I'd like to say I was up early the next morning making coffee and scrambling eggs, charming my way to Jax's heart, but the truth was that when I awoke, Jax was already dressing. I stretched in the bed and smiled, feeling the heavy, decadent pleasure from the night before still settling in my limbs. "Morning."

He grinned as he pulled on his sweater. "Morning, coffee girl."

I brought the sheet up across my breasts, suddenly self-conscious of my nakedness. The sun was just starting to streak through the blinds in the window. My heart sagged. "You're leaving already?"

"I have to go back to the inn to shower," he smiled. "I'll bring a change of clothes next time."

Next time. There was a nice thought. I leaned back against the pillow, still fuzzy from the rush of our time together. Or maybe that was from the lack of sleep, because if I had invited Jax to spend the night with the expectation that we'd sleep, he'd shown me the error of my ways. Then again, I'd been happily complicit.

He pressed one hand against the wall and leaned forward to give me a slow, drowsy kiss on the lips. "Will I see you later?" I asked.

"Depends on whether you want me around."

I reached forward to drag my fingers down his sweater. "I do."

"Then I'll be wherever you are." He kissed me on the cheek and righted himself. "I'll see you on set. Unless you want a ride?"

"I'll catch a ride with Emily."

I watched him walk out of the bedroom and moments later, I heard him shut the door behind him. The clock read four thirty. Time to get up.

I showered quickly, dressed, and returned to Hedda's. Jessie was just coming down the stairs from her apartment, clutching a thermos. She narrowed her gaze at me. "What are you so pleased about?"

"Nothing," I said, trying to sound nonchalant and failing miserably. Maybe I'm good at faking certain things. My talents end at deceiving my cousin. She can see straight through me.

Jessie reached the bottom of the stairs. Her straight brown hair fell to her shoulders, still damp. "Jax forgot his sports car last night," she mused as she took a sip from the thermos. "It was still parked on the street when I got up this morning."

"Huh. Weird."

She smirked and unlocked the door to the bakery. "You're the only one who thinks so."

We loaded the trays of food into the van without talking, and I figured I was going to get away without having to explain myself. Just as we were shutting the back doors to the van, Jessie said, "Still think my truffles are better than sex?"

My pulse kicked into high gear at the thought of the night before, of Jax's body and whispers, and the thought that one of the biggest stars in Hollywood had seduced *me*. My skin was flushed, but I couldn't wipe the grin off my face. "I'm reconsidering my position. I may have spoken too soon."

"Ha! I thought so." Jessie chuckled and jabbed a finger against my chest. "You owe me details. None of this 'don't kiss and tell' crap."

"Fine. Just don't tell Dad anything, promise?"

"Gross! Like I'd ever."

Emily emerged from the bakery with a smile that was too bright for the hour. "Ready?"

I glanced at Jessie, who quipped, "Your chariot awaits."

Emily didn't know, and I didn't tell her. As we drove to Great Barrington, I reveled in my secret until I remembered that I'd promised to run lines with Griff. Nothing like seeing your ex-boyfriend to take the shine off a great fling.

My stomach sparked at the thought. "Fling" — was that what it was? And from that little kernel sprouted a crop of self-doubt and dread. I'd gone from being a self-respecting woman to Jax's latest conquest. I felt sick. Reality is an ugly, ugly thing.

CHAPTER FOURTEEN

THE CLOSER WE got to the set, the more I believed that I'd made a mistake by spending the night with Jax. He wasn't interested in me beyond acquiring another trophy. The more I thought about it, the more it made sense that he'd want me to believe he had real feelings for me, because then wouldn't I develop real feelings for *him*? I could just imagine the photographs caught by the paparazzi: me gazing adoringly into Jax's eyes. His agent and publicist would love that. As incredible as the night had been, I could no longer think about it without wanting to cry. He'd made a fool out of me. Even worse, I'd helped.

I fumed for a while, waiting in the trailer for him to appear and convince me that I was mistaken and that our shared night had actually meant something. When he didn't, I stormed away to Griff's trailer and vowed that it would remain my deep, dark, pathetic secret that I'd allowed Jax Cosgrove to break my heart. Griff had dumped me in public and across the tabloids. I wouldn't allow Jax to know how he'd hurt me.

When I arrived at the trailer, Griff answered the door shirtless, leaning against the doorjamb so that his arm fell over his head, his other arm hidden behind the door. He gave me a sexy, lopsided grin. I know what he'd intended for me to think, but all that kept running through my mind was that he'd waxed his chest, and it looked odd. "Hey, Wren," he purred. "You're early."

I was ten minutes late. "Did I catch you at a bad time?"

The grin deepened, showing off that dimple in his right cheek. "Not at all. Come on in." He stepped aside to allow me entrance. "I was just about to make some coffee. Would you like some?"

"I'm all right, thanks."

"You sure?" He picked up his cell. "I'm going to call that PA. What's his name — George." He gave me a knowing look. "The one that was bothering you yesterday."

"He really wasn't —"

He pressed a finger to my lips, holding the cell phone to his ear. "Shh. We both know what was going on there."

I was about to defend poor George when Griff said, "Heya, George? It's Griff. Can you bring two coffees and some breakfast to my trailer?" He winked at me and my skin crawled. What had I seen in this guy? "Yeah, bring an assortment of whatever they have. Definitely some hard-boiled eggs. Bottled water. May as well bring some juice, too. I have company, and I want to make sure I have something she likes."

My mouth was half-open. Had he always been this gross? He disconnected the call and smiled as if he'd actually accomplished something worth feeling superior about. "Breakfast will be here in fifteen minutes. Make yourself comfortable in the meantime."

I released a deep breath that failed to drag my mounting tension with it and sat back on the couch. "Maybe we should just run our lines."

"All right." He pulled on a red Henley that had been lying across the back of a chair. Show's over, I thought as his bare chest disappeared from view. Then he sat next to me. *Right* next to me.

The scene was simple. We were paired in a straightforward romantic subplot: I was a woman in the marketing department, and he was the hunk in the mailroom that all the women in the office building secretly drooled over. In this scene, we were getting to know each other for the first time, and we happened to be stuck in an elevator.

I opened my script to the right page and set it on my lap. "So, we're trapped in an elevator."

"Help! I'm in an elevator!" He laughed and flailed his hands, pantomiming walls.

My stomach tilted in that way it does when someone tries too hard to be funny. I forced a polite laugh. "Right." I turned the page. "You have the first line."

"I do?" He craned his neck to read over my shoulder. "I thought you did."

I pointed to the page. "Right there. You're supposed to say, 'This can't be happening.' Then *I* say, 'Did you press the button? They were fixing the elevator earlier; it can't be broken again already.'"

"Huh." He snaked his hand behind me and tickled his fingers against the back of my neck. "Is that what it says?"

I scooted over and shut the screenplay. "I don't think you're serious about reading lines."

"I'm serious, I'm serious." He smiled sadly. "I guess I'm feeling a little distracted, that's all. This is going to sound strange, but I guess I can't believe you're actually here. With me." His right hand crept closer to mine. "I made some mistakes, and you have every reason to hate me, but...I miss you. You look so...great. Different, somehow."

"Griff." I pulled my hand back, trying not to look as repulsed as I was feeling. "What about Poppy?"

His lower lip jutted as he sat back in his seat. "We're over. She's not even returning my texts."

I thumbed the pages of the screenplay. "Maybe we should just run our lines."

My attempt to redirect the conversation fell flat. "Can I tell you something?"

He shifted his body and pulled closer to my side. I would have backed away, except I was blocked by the arm of the couch. "Okay."

"Poppy and I — we were nothing. We had a relationship that a lot of people probably wouldn't understand. A relationship that had more to do with appearances than feelings. Does that make sense?"

Until that moment, whenever I'd heard someone say that their blood had started to boil, I thought it was hyperbole. It turns out I simply lacked imagination, because when Griff started to explain his relationship with Poppy, I felt the blood in my veins begin a rapid simmer that threatened to spill over the edge. I was fighting so hard to not jump up and run right then and there that I could barely muster the energy to reply, "Oh?"

He groaned into his hand. "Now wait. Don't tell me you're going to do that thing where you get upset at me, okay? Because I'm being honest. That's a good thing."

I gritted my teeth and tightened my hands into fists, the better to pummel him with if he tried to make a pass at me. "You cheated. You don't get to tell me how to feel about it."

With a heavy sigh, he flung one arm across the back of the couch. "I guess that's fair. It's only — I got caught up in the sudden fame. I was thinking of my career, and I made a mistake." He glanced at me. "We were great together. I see that now."

I turned away. "So you and Poppy — what was the arrangement?"

He sat back with a heavy exhalation and folded his hands behind his head. "Strictly business. I was going places, and I needed to be seen with someone like her. She needed the same. It was totally wrong of me. Stupid. I was taking advice from the wrong people. And I'm sorry. Wren?" He made a grab for my hand, which I yanked away. "I'm sorry. It was a relationship of convenience, nothing real. I thought you should know that."

Wait, he was kidding me. He had to have figured out that Jax and I were engaged in a relationship of the same sort…right? But as I darted my gaze across his face, I saw that he was completely serious. There wasn't a trace of humor or irony in those eyes or in the straight set of his lips. "Relationships come in all shapes and sizes," I replied. I'd heard the same uttered many times by a guest psychologist on a particular talk show. Coming from my mouth, it sounded even more trite.

I folded my hands together in my lap, grinding my fingernails into my flesh. "It's over. I've moved on. Don't worry about it."

"Exactly. See, I knew you'd understand." He leaned back on the couch as if that were that.

"I've been in relationships of convenience, too," I said.

Something in my voice may have tipped him off, because he lowered his when he said, "What about Jax?"

"No. Not Jax. We're the real thing. For sure."

He didn't look convinced. Maybe he was convinced enough but undeterred, because he budged barely an inch. "Lucky Jax," he whispered.

"Yep."

He paused to rub at the side of his face before saying, "Maybe we weren't exactly perfect together." He looked at me then. "You never really got me, you know?"

What the ever-loving —? I was choking on my own rage. Seeing the proverbial red, the whole thing. So I had never gotten him? What about all of those kale smoothies I'd consumed in solidarity when he was dropping a few pounds for a screen test? What about when I'd picked up extra hours at a part-time job — my second job, mind you — so Griff could spend more time auditioning?

I realized my hands were locked in tight fists, and I rapped them against my thighs and forced a laugh that didn't sound at all good-natured. Then again, Griff wasn't one to notice these things.

"There are always two sides to every story," I said through clenched teeth. It was another insight I'd heard on that talk show from that same psychologist. I made a note to watch better television. "But I don't want to revisit this."

"Oh sure. I can't say I'm perfect either," he laughed easily. "Too much time in the weight room."

A loud laugh burst from my throat. "Ah yes, the weight room. I'm sure if I racked my brain in search of your imperfections, I'd cite *that* first. The fact that you cheated would come a distant second."

He blinked and turned away. "I see you're angry, but I apologized for cheating already."

"Oh for the love of —" I rose to my feet and rolled the screenplay, then pointed it at him. "I don't want to talk about our relationship. I came here to run lines. When you're ready to do that —"

"Poppy used me."

The words fell out, pressed by anger that was almost palpable. I opened my mouth, closed it. Opened it again and said, "Sorry?"

"I'd been cast in Brennan's movie, and she knew it. It's like she was first in line to see if she could get something from me, and I was stupid enough to fall for it." He drew his fingers through his hair. "Who was she? Just some girl from a reality television show. Then we started dating and the offers came in. Commercials. Cosmetics. Film. It was all because she was linked to *me*." He jabbed at his chest with his index finger. "And then what does she do? She goes and tries to find something better."

Now I was all ears, and it was my turn to shift closer. "Poppy...cheated on you."

His jaw tightened. "I just found out about it last week. She told me at the party. Can you imagine?" He shook his head. "She made this big scene, threw that engagement ring...I don't even know where. No one's found it. Do you know how much it cost me? A *lot*."

213

"She told you before she threw the ring?"

"After. After you saved her from the pool. I went over to check on her, and she said it matter-of-factly."

My breath was lighter. I couldn't miss a single word of this. "What, exactly, did she say to you?"

"I asked her if she was all right. And I wanted to make sure she knew I hadn't pushed her." He looked at me with a shrug. "With Pops, you never knew what she was going to get in her head."

"And what did she say?"

"After I told her I hadn't pushed her, she looked at me, all calm, and said, 'I've been seeing someone else.' Then she got up and left the party. Same way you did, but without the running. If you ask me," Griff said glumly, "she ran off with him, whoever he is. That's where she is now, and we'll all hear about it soon enough. She's determined to make a fool out of me."

He set his head in his hands, and for a glimmer of a nanosecond, I considered reaching over and telling him the truth. That Poppy had cheated on him with Hodges Brennan, who'd used *her*, and given her a second-rate role in this very movie. It was like everyone had gotten their comeuppance, and it was all going to be all right. But that's not much consolation, and if I felt Griff's pain, it was only because he'd subjected me to the same public humiliation. I bit my lip and then said, "That kind of thing hurts like hell, doesn't it?"

"Yeah."

"It will get better. Trust me."

There was a knock on the door, and we heard George's voice announce, "Mr. Dannel? Your breakfast, sir."

I patted him on the shoulder. "We should eat. I'm starving."

I rose and went to the door, leaving Griff sitting alone on the couch. They say revenge is a dish best served cold, but maybe I'm too much of a softie. Griff had done his share of damage, but being cheated on? It's not something I'd even wish on *him*.

George entered with two small trays, one teeming with scones and muffins Jessie, Cash and I had baked last night, the other piled with small bowls of hard-boiled eggs, bacon and sausage. Griff's trailer was fancier than mine, and he had plenty of space for the trays. After a quick run back to his cart, George returned with two coffees in his hand. "Thanks, George," I said with a big smile.

"Anything else, Ms. Mallory?"

"That's all for now." I nudged the door closed with the toe of my left shoe and studied Griff's sad figure, still slumped on the couch. Without a word, I opened his coffee and added two packets of sugar. Then I replaced the lid and held it out to him. "Here. Chin up."

Griff had a sad look on his face. "You still remember that I take two sugars in my coffee."

"Yeah. I've made you a lot of coffee." I eased into the seat beside him and patted him on the shoulder. "Look, we're over. As in, *over*. Forever. You cheated on me and it

215

was awful, and I have a shred of self-respect. But life is cruel, and now we're in this movie together and so we have to pretend to like each other. But Griff? It's purely make-believe, okay? The last thing I want is to get dragged into whatever jealousy-inducing scheme you have to get back at Poppy."

He turned his gaze to his steaming coffee and nodded solemnly. "All right."

"Wonderful." I smoothed my screenplay on my lap. "Let's run some lines, shall we?"

When I came back to my trailer, Jax was sitting on the front steps. He struck a match as I approached and held it up, watching me as I passed him and unlocked the door. "Where've you been? I was waiting."

I wrinkled my nose. "Are you an arsonist now?" With a quick breath, he blew out the flame and tossed the match to the asphalt. "Jeez, why don't you just litter the ground with some empties while you're at it?"

"I haven't had a drink in two weeks, sweet cheeks." He eased off the steps and collected the wooden stubs he'd thrown to the ground. "I'm not burning your charming dressing room, don't worry. I'm not a complete wretch."

He certainly didn't look like a wretch in his form-fitting charcoal tee. His dark hair was tousled, and he hadn't bothered to shave. He looked a little dirty. My eyes instantly went to his mouth — that wicked half-smirk that told me that he was thinking exactly what I was thinking. I looked away.

"An icy reception if I've ever seen one," he muttered to himself as he shut the door. "I was hoping we'd moved past all of this."

"All of what?" I pretended to be interested in the makeup on the desk.

"Your disdain for me." He actually sounded injured as he lay back on the couch. "I couldn't find you anywhere. No note. No reply to my texts."

"Sorry, I was with Griff, running lines. We're shooting a scene today."

"Oh." He was silent for a long time before he said, "How did that go?"

I picked up the eyeshadow brush, then tossed it back down to the table again. All of my resolve to distance myself from him, right up in smoke with a simple question. "God, Jax. I feel like I'm losing my mind right now. Why is that?"

"Fatigue. Drugs. General dramatic tendencies. One of them or in combination." He rested his arm beneath his head. "Was it that hard for you, to see Griff?"

"Not as hard as I thought it would be. It's been months now. I moved across the country, restarted my life. I'm over him."

Jax scratched at the spot above his bicep, where the tattoo circled his arm. "Griff's an idiot," he said. "He doesn't know what he lost."

My traitorous heart warmed ever so slightly. I turned my chair to look at him. "Thanks," I murmured. His tattoo caught my eye. "What's that design on your arm about, anyway?"

He pulled it back to look at it as if he needed to remember himself. "Chains," he said. "All the chains from the past. But see —" He turned his arm around. "They're broken. That's my future, right there."

"I like that. Chains of the past. Mistakes?"

"Mistakes. Origins." He kept his gaze fixed on the ceiling. "I was raised by a single mom, me and my brother. We were on food stamps, but that wasn't enough some days. We were hungry a lot. But now..."

He didn't finish the sentence. He was driving a Maserati around Archer Cove, hanging out on movie sets, and attending A-list parties. He was on the short list to be cast as the leading actor in what would surely be one of the biggest hits of the following year. "Now it's all different."

"Yeah. It should be, but deep down it's all the same. I'm still the same kid." He turned his head to look at me. "I used to wash dishes at a diner. I was twelve years old but I told them I was sixteen. They didn't ask for proof. It gave us grocery money, and I worked there for years. I eventually advanced to waitstaff. It's where I met the agent who gave me my break." He released a soft breath. "My mom is proud. She didn't like that I was working like that, so when I gave her that money, I told her it wasn't for food. I told her I was buying her a house. Last year, I finally did. Right on the beach, where she always wanted to be."

"Wow." I let it all sink in. "You're a real success story."

Jax had overcome so many odds — many more than I had. He might have a few rough edges, but I couldn't help but admire him. Not like my admiration meant anything. He set one foot on the arm of the couch and allowed the other to drop to the floor beside him.

"I'm some kind of story," he said. He paused. "What's wrong today, Wren? If it's about your performance last night, trust me — you were amazing."

My cheeks began to smolder. "No. Why does your mind always go there?"

"Why should it go anywhere else?" He grinned, taking obvious pleasure in my discomfort. "It's just that you surprise me. When I bring a woman to climax multiple times over the evening, she doesn't normally give me that 'drop dead' glare that you're giving me now."

"Good God." I smoothed my hands across my face. "You make me feel like a Puritan sometimes, the way you talk."

"Yes. I'm *honest*." He slid off the couch and stepped forward, dropping to one knee and slinging an arm across the back of my chair. "And when I said you were amazing, I meant it. And when I say that we should do it again —" He lifted my hand and pressed a kiss into the backs of my fingers. "That's because I want to."

I couldn't deny the surge he sent through me, or the steady hammering of my heart. My body had all but surrendered to him, loosening inch my inch as he trailed his hand higher up my thighs. "Jax. This is supposed to be pretend."

"Does this feel pretend to you?" His voice was heavy with arousal. It was a non-answer, but my brain had shut off. He was teasing off my skirt, and I didn't feel like arguing about it.

CHAPTER FIFTEEN

I ARRIVED ON set at one o'clock, but we didn't get shooting until nearly three. I'd heard horror stories about Alex Sherapovna, that he was a director obsessed with details, that it wasn't uncommon for him to require even the best actors to shoot a scene fifty times before he was satisfied. We must have gotten lucky, because he only made Griff and me shoot the brief elevator scene twenty-three times. Even then, I was nearly weeping with frustration by the end.

The scene ended with Griff pinning me to the wall of the elevator, my bare leg wrapped around his waist. "I don't see anything wrong with getting a little dirty while we're here, do you?" I crooned.

"And cut!" Alex called. "That's a wrap. Great job, you two."

I lowered my leg and released my grip on Griff. "Thank God."

"You're a natural," Griff smiled at me and gave me a clap on the back like we were old friends. Which we were, I suppose. "I really like the rawness you bring."

I had no idea what that meant, and I was operating on such little sleep that my patience was a small worn-out stub of what it usually was. "Thanks," I nearly growled. Someone waved at me from across the room. "I think I see my agent. I have to go talk to her."

"Sure. See you tomorrow."

I didn't even reply, instead working my way through the maze of people, wires, and machinery. Greta grabbed my hand when she saw me and led me to the side. "Look at you, Wren. Acting genius." She squeezed my hand. "What did I always tell you?"

"You said I should act," I mumbled, and unscrewed the cap from the bottle of water she'd handed me.

"I told you you'd be great, and holy cow." She beamed. "I'm brilliant."

I took a long drink, finishing off the water. My head had started to pound, and I was achy from fatigue. "I don't know how people keep up with these hours."

"Most people on set aren't pulling a night shift at a bakery the way you are." She smoothed my hair and adjusted the collar on my blouse affectionately. "Come on. You're finished for the day, right?"

"Yeah." Thank goodness. Brennan must have pulled some strings for me, because the crew was preparing to shoot yet another scene, and filming would go late into the night. "I have a few more scenes tomorrow, but it's really a small part."

"But you're going to be great." She slipped her arm around my waist as we walked out. "You really are a natural. Of course, I knew this."

"I've gotta get out of here. Jessie's probably waiting for me." The guilt tugged at me as I pictured my cousin and dad baking alone. Jax had come to the shoot with me, but I noticed with a tug of disappointment that he'd left. I sighed, feeling a dark cloud cross over my mood. "This schedule is wearing on me."

"Funny you should say that, because I was just talking to Rubee Adams, you know, from Celebrity Burn? Poppy checked in this morning." Greta stopped and gave a little wave to a woman who looked familiar. "There's Rubee. She'll tell you." She pasted a smile on her face and waved merrily. "Rubee! Have you met Wren yet?"

Gwen's left hand pushed me forward so hard that I nearly stumbled into Rubee's arms. She was wearing several gold bracelets on each wrist, and they clattered with every movement. "I *have* met Wren," she cooed. "We saw each other at Hodges Brennan's party, I believe. She gave me a juicy piece of gossip." She winked at me, and my cheeks burned at the memory of my whopper about Jax's waxing habits. Not my brightest moment, by a long shot. "How are you?"

"Great." I inhaled the scent of her stifling perfume. It smelled like a summer garden in a tightly closed space on a brutally hot day. "Just…everything's so *great*."

"Wren's been concerned about Poppy." Greta smoothed a lock of my hair affectionately behind my ear.

"Concerned about Poppy?" Rubee tilted her head in confusion, and at that moment I felt like I was up to my waist in lies and deception and half-truths, and this territory was getting much too bizarre to navigate.

"Yeah, I just..." I scratched at my arm, wilting under her sharp gaze. "You know, I pulled her out of the pool and she didn't sound like she was doing well. She said something to me — privately — that made me concerned that she was having a difficult time with something."

"Oh," Rubee nodded as if my vague response explained everything. "Yes. She has been going through some transitions, poor dear. But I think she's doing much better now. She's off in Fiji. She says she has no plans to return any time soon." She giggled. "Of course, we know better, right, Greta? We know Poppy. Can you say 'workaholic'?"

I shifted my weight as they shared a laugh about Poppy's work ethic. My head was throbbing now. So this was Poppy's story, that she was in Fiji? I needed to lie down somewhere and not think about anything for a good, long while. "So she's sending you updates about her getaway?" I said. "That's good she's enjoying herself."

"'Enjoying herself' is an understatement. Poor girl needed a break." Rubee sighed and shook her head. "If you ask me, she's checked herself into some kind of treatment program, though they don't normally let them use electronic devices."

"You think she's in rehab?" I started. "What for?"

"Oh, who knows. Pills. Drugs. Booze. Sex addiction seems common these days, but that doesn't usually make you fall in a swimming pool." Rubee licked the tip of her finger before smoothing down one eyebrow. "An impromptu trip to Fiji doesn't seem like Poppy's style. She's tightly wound, if you know what I mean. She's the type to plan to be spontaneous. But she says she's in Fiji so that's what I'm going to report." She gave me a wink. "That's what you get when you have a relationship with me, Wren: the benefit of the doubt."

"A relationship?"

I could tell from Rubee's eye roll that this was a horrifying response. "Oh jeezus, Greta. How green *is* she?" She turned back to me and took a step closer, overwhelming me with the smell of hot flowers again. "You know how reporters get information, right, honey? They have sources. Anonymous sources, usually. I operate the same exact way. People tell me things and I report on it. They keep coming back because I always make good on my promises. One," she held up a finger, "I don't attach names to stories. Two, I pay well."

Greta eyed me sidelong. "Rubee pays in notoriety," she explained. "Not the same as cash."

"Better than cash," Rubee said. "Do you know how many hits I get on Celebrity Burn? Millions. I'm known for having the inside scoop, for being the first to report. Placement on my site can make or break a star." She pursed her lips at me, reaching out to stroke the hem of my blouse. "Case in point. I meet a young starlet at a house party. She gives me some interesting gossip about a hot young man she's in a relationship with, and then she jumps, fully clothed, into a swimming pool to save another young starlet from drowning. Naturally I find this to be fascinating." She smiled slyly. "So I run a story about her heroics the next day. She's someone I want my readers to watch. Other bloggers pick up the story — who *is* this mystery woman? Why hasn't anyone heard about her before? They want to know more. They're clamoring for pictures, which start to surface. She's cozy with Jax Cosgrove on the beach, they're walking hand in hand in a charming little seaside town. Suddenly she's been offered a role in a film that Hodges Brennan is producing. Poof!" She snapped her fingers. "She's a star."

There were a hundred questions running across my aching head, not the least of which was why someone like Rubee would choose to construct a celebrity out of me. I was a nobody, officially. But mostly, I couldn't dwell on it. I had only a night of baking to look forward to, a few hours of sleep, and then another day on set where I'd pretend to be dating a man for whom I had developed some very real feelings.

"We appreciate everything you've done for her," Greta said, filling the silence. "You basically discovered her!"

She laughed, but I felt sick to my stomach. I was living in a different universe, officially.

"I know star quality when I see it," Rubee said. "So tell me, Wren: what's the word on set? Anything interesting happening?"

I fumbled for an answer. "I, uh…I have to think about it."

"Come on now. *Nothing* springs to mind?"

Rubee sidled closer to my side. Around us, the random crew member passed, carrying a camera or sound equipment, the occasional rope or ladder, but they kept their distance. No one was listening in.

I looked at Rubee, really studying her tiny gray eyes and her red-stained lips. Her hair was a deep shade of reddish maroon bordering on purple. Beneath the pale foundation layered on her skin, I noticed freckles that looked an awful lot like my own — buried, sure, but there. "Is Poppy selling you secrets?" I barely breathed the words. I didn't consider the question before I spoke. I asked the question because I had to know.

In a flash, I knew I'd underestimated Rubee. A hardness closed around her eyes, or maybe it was there before and I hadn't noticed it until that moment. It made no difference, because in a blink of an eye, everything between us changed. Rubee believed she'd made me a star, and I'd shown ingratitude. Then, just as quickly as it had arrived, the moment passed and Rubee was back to herself.

"Poppy and I speak all the time," she said breezily.

"That's not what I mean. Does she give you stories for your blog?"

"I told you, I don't name names." Rubee smiled unpleasantly. "I take it that means you don't have anything new for me to add to my site?"

The icy tone of her voice sent goose pimples crawling across my skin. I may have been a complete fraud, but even I wouldn't stoop to selling gossip and secrets in exchange for free publicity. "Yeah," I said. "That's a good way to take it."

She pinched her lips and gave me a hard stare. "Too bad. I may not have anything nice to say about you anymore. *Wren.*"

Something about the way my name rang from her mouth sent a shiver up my spine, but I tried not to let it show that she'd affected me. Instead, I shrugged and brushed past her. "I've got plans. Sorry to run."

Behind me, I heard Greta muttering some frantic apologies, but I didn't hear anything from Rubee. I'd never felt so wrung out in my life, and I wasn't quite sure who I even was any longer. Under the circumstances, it was hard to care what anyone else thought of me.

"Wren! Over here!"

I turned to see Jax standing by a golf cart, wearing a big smile. My mood brightened. "Jax."

"Sorry I missed the end. I wanted to get you this." He handed me a giant bottle of spring water. "Come on. I'll give you a ride home."

"I'm heading to work at Hedda's."

"Then I'll give you a ride there." He smiled and wrapped his arm around my shoulders, pulling me closer to his side and kissing the top of my head. "Go get changed. I'll meet you at the car."

I flung my arms around his waist and buried my face in his chest. His shirt was soft against my cheek, but below it was the hard wall of his abdomen. We stood there for a moment as I allowed the rest of the world to slip away. Let Jessie and Dad wait a few more minutes. Right then, Jax was all I needed.

CHAPTER SIXTEEN

I REALIZED WHEN the smell of fresh paint greeted me at the door that renovations were already underway in the bakery. I walked through the kitchen toward the main dining area and saw the evidence: a large canvas drop cloth spread across the tiles and my mom standing on a wooden stepladder, rolling light-green paint down the wall. Two of the college students Dad had hired for the summer were helping. "What do you think?" Jessie asked.

The color Mom had selected reminded me faintly of an opal. "I didn't realize how dirty the white paint was."

"That was my thought, too," Jessie said. "The whole space will look so much cleaner when they're finished."

"This isn't the end of it," Mom promised, speaking into the wall as she focused. "I've got plans. I'm having sea glass subway tiles installed behind the counter. We're freshening up the wrought-iron tables. You won't be able to recognize the place when I'm finished."

The small team had already managed to cover almost half of the wall space, and it was still dinnertime. "Are you finishing the painting tonight?"

"That's the plan," Mom said.

"They have to," Dad corrected as he came into the room with a few bags of day-old pastries. "It's bad enough the place is going to smell like a chemical factory. I can't have it looking half-painted, too."

Mom casually rolled her brush into the paint tin, amusement seeping into her face. "I told you it would be finished on time, Hank. I'll stay here all night if I have to. And I also told you that this is a low-odor paint. Your customers are still going to be able to smell your coffee cake."

I braced myself for Dad's sharp retort, one in which he reiterated to Mom how serious he was about his business, but that reply never came. Instead, Dad walked over to stand just behind her ladder, watching the color spread across the wall. "You sure that ladder is safe, Lil? It's old."

"It's fine," she replied lightly. "You always worried too much."

"I can't help it." He shifted his weight from one foot to the other. "Here, let me check it. If you come down for a minute — I can do it quickly."

"Hank." Mom stopped and turned to face him. "I'm twelve inches off the ground. Even if I fell, I'd be fine. Stop worrying."

Here we go, I thought. This could get ugly, with Dad reminding Mom that this was his ladder and he knew for darn sure it was unstable. Then Mom would remind Dad that interior design was *her* business, and she knew darn well what she was doing. Then they would rehash every painful part of their past so that everyone who worked in the bakery would hear it, and if I was really lucky, they'd discuss my upbringing and whether or not I was living to my potential, and who should take blame for which of my shortcomings.

But that's not what happened. Instead, they locked gazes, and then they smiled at each other. "I worry. I can't help it," Dad muttered.

"I know," Mom said warmly. "It's sweet."

The gaze lingered, and then she turned back to the wall. Dad walked past me and headed into the kitchen, leaving Jessie and me standing agape. She spoke first. "What just happened there?"

My brain was short-circuiting, the thoughts misfiring in random order. "Worry. Not fighting. Oh my God." I looked at my cousin. "Did they just flirt?"

No. This was not flirting or any kind of shared concern. I mean, they'd gotten divorced how long ago? And in all of those years, there had never been any sniff of a reunion. "Maybe your dad is just really excited about new paint," Jessie whispered in that diplomatic voice that made it clear she didn't believe a word she'd just said. "It's been a long time since we've had new paint in here."

"Yes. It's the fumes," I agreed. Sure, I'd seen one or two movies about divorced parents falling back in love against all odds, but I was rounding the bend to thirty years old. That should have happened when I was still a teenager. "I just can't process this right now," I said, and headed back into the kitchen.

"Better to not think about it," Jessie said. Then added, "But it would be great, right? If they got back together? It's probably the paint fumes, though."

"Probably."

There was a knock and I looked up to see Jax smiling at me through the screen door. I nearly sprinted to let him in, grateful for the distraction from the bizarre exchange I'd just witnessed. "I hope you brought your painting clothes," I said. "Mom's out there on the stepladder."

He glanced down at his jeans and black polo. Definitely not ready to paint, but still pretty hot. "Does she need help? I can get changed —"

"It won't take much longer," Dad boomed from across the kitchen. He nodded at a standing mixer. "If you're here to work, I've got a batch of cinnamon rolls with your name on it."

Jax looked at me. "I can do that, Mr. Mallory." We watched as Dad left the room, and then Jax touched my arm lightly and lowered his voice. "You're baking too, right?"

My fingers flew recklessly to grab at one of his belt loops, tugging him closer. I wondered how it was possible to have had so much of one person and to still want more. "I'm baking too," I whispered. "By the way, you owe me a bicycle. Don't think I've forgotten."

"I would never think such a thing."

"I hope you brought your little sports car."

He leaned closer, his face falling in shadow. "You need another ride?"

The innuendo sent the breath shooting straight out of my lungs, and I nodded helplessly. "Uh huh." Did I ever.

He pulled himself to his full height, hovering over me, and said, "Well. I'll see what I can do." Then he gave a cheeky wink that sent the blood rushing straight from my head.

I reached out with one hand, gripping the counter to steady myself. For God's sake, I was a virtual puddle of frenzied hormones. I collected myself just in time to look up and see Jessie observing me with a subtle arch of one eyebrow. I shook my head at her and mouthed, *Don't*.

She dropped her jaw in mock horror and mouthed back, *Me?* Then she returned to her work, a Cheshire Cat grin on her face.

With Jax's extra help, Dad, Emily, Jessie and I were able to finish the evening's baking earlier than usual. We were cleaning up when Mom entered the kitchen and announced, "Done."

Her hands and clothing were splattered with paint, and a streak of green raced up her cheek. She looked proud and tired, and even though there were five of us in the kitchen, her gaze was fixed squarely on Dad, who was taking unusual care arranging a platter of muffins. "What's that?" he asked.

Mom sighed and set her hands on her hips. "I'm done with the paint. You should come out and see it."

"In a minute," Dad said, shifting a blueberry cobbler muffin he'd just set in place a moment ago slightly to the side. "We're almost finished."

"I want to see it," I said. I untied my apron and hung it on a hook. My hands were still covered in flour, but I wasn't about to go groping the wall.

"I'm coming too," Jessie said.

Jax and Emily followed us into the bakery. Mom, from whom I'd clearly inherited my flair for the dramatic, had turned off the lights before gathering us. "Ready?" she asked as we stood in the darkness. She flipped the light switch with a loud, "Ta-da!"

Amazing what a coat of fresh paint could do. The white trim looked whiter, the room looked larger, and even the light fell differently. "Ignore the floor tiles for now," Mom said. "I promise they'll look much better in a few days. But doesn't it look fabulous?"

"I love it!" Jessie gasped. "It looks so clean."

"It's like a new space," Emily agreed. "Beautiful."

"Isn't it?" Mom crossed her arms across her chest. "I'm pleased." She looked over our heads. "Nice of you to join us, Hank."

Dad mumbled something behind us and then stopped. "Wow. This actually looks great."

Mom's short brown hair was pulled into a ponytail, but she tucked a loose strand behind her ear. "You had your doubts?"

He tilted his head as he looked at her. "I shouldn't have." He gazed around the room. "This is the perfect color for this space."

Mom crossed her ankles demurely and looked down at the floor.

Okay, now this was getting weird. They were smiling at each other and being so friendly and supportive that it was starting to make my skin crawl. "It's super, Mom. Nice job." I pointed back to the kitchen. "I'm going to get cleaning up. It's been a long day."

"Sure, honey," Mom said. "I'll just remove this tape and head home. I have a client meeting in the morning."

Behind me, Jessie, Dad, and Emily offered to help her. There were still some dishes piled up beside the sink, though. Someone had to take care of those. I reached for a bowl when Jax came up behind me and whispered, "Let's go."

He wrapped one hand across my stomach and reached the other down my side. A shiver darted across my skin as he pressed his warm lips to my jaw. "I...can't," I nearly moaned. "I have to help clean up." His fingers trailed a thread of fire across my back. "I'll do it quickly."

"I'll help."

I can't say those dishes sparkled when we were through with them, but they were clean enough. All the time, Jax made a point of brushing up against me, standing close enough that I could feel his body heat. I swept a rag across the counters quickly and muttered a quick good-bye to my family. I'd have some explaining to do to Jessie, but my mind was on other matters.

It turns out the walk home takes forever when you stop in every dark shadow to kiss. I fell in love with his arms and back, with feeling the strength of his muscles below my fingers. He pressed me up against a wooden fence and kissed me deeply, his strong hands pulling my waist closer to his. "Wren," he groaned into my ear. "Do you know what you do to me?"

I closed my eyes, allowing my senses to be filled with him. The smell of his spicy cologne, the feel of his warmth, the sound of his breath, the taste of his lips. I reached up to touch his chest and felt his heart nearly escape from its confines. "Come on," I whispered. "We're almost there."

We barely made it, clambering up the back stairs to my apartment. I unlocked the door with trembling fingers, struggling to gather my breath. The fish fryers at Crabby Andy's were going at full blast and my apartment stunk, but I didn't care. From that point on, the smell of fried food would secretly remind me of Jax's skillful hands and the thrilling delirium of that long, sleepless night.

CHAPTER SEVENTEEN

IF I'D EVER thought I was in love before, I'd been wrong. This was different. I couldn't get the smile off my face, and I didn't even care.

"Oh my," Jessie commented when she saw me the next morning. "Things are getting serious."

They didn't feel serious. They felt…blissfully light and pleasant, even with the overcast morning. "Good morning," was all I replied.

Jessie burst out laughing. "Yes, from the looks of it."

We loaded the van and Emily and I set off to the movie set, parking the van in the usual spot. Lou wasn't waiting, so I walked the distance to my trailer. I needed the time to think. I grabbed a small plate of muffins to share with Jax and a cup of coffee for myself. I was so lost in thought that I didn't notice the figure sitting on the steps to the trailer until I'd nearly stepped on him. "Cash," I gasped. "What are you doing here?"

Reflexively, I held out the plate of muffins. He selected cranberry white chocolate chip while eyeing me coolly, like he was imagining himself to be a hotshot television detective. "Ms. Mallory. You're up early."

"'Ms. Mallory'? We were lab partners in chemistry, Cash. Also, I gave you a muffin." I set one foot on the stairs to the trailer and leaned against the handrail. "I'm here early because Hedda's is catering the set. I'm not getting much sleep these days." To illustrate, I took a sip of my coffee. Yikes — too hot. The tip of my tongue went numb.

"Sorry. You're right. It's just..." He paused and scrunched his face so that I could actually watch him collect his thoughts. "Look at all of the good fortune that came your way when Poppy Hayes disappeared: a role in a movie, a catering contract. And your ex-boyfriend is available again." He lifted his shoulders helplessly. "I've got to follow the leads."

"I understand. Mind if I eat?" I broke off a piece of a blueberry cobbler muffin without waiting for permission. "Look, I've told you everything I know about Poppy. Griff's not too broken up about it, either, but he didn't have anything to do with anything."

He pulled himself to his feet and struck a pose, resting one arm against the handrail. "But you see what kind of position I'm in? I like you, Wren, but from what I can see, you're the only person who's benefitted from Poppy's murder."

I coughed on my muffin, sending little crumbs flying. A few landed on Cash's shirt, and I watched him wipe them away. "Murder? Why do you think she's dead?"

"No one's heard from her." He folded his ham hocks across his chest and lifted his chin. "You seem surprised by that."

"Uh, *yeah*," I managed through the remaining muffin in my mouth. "Have you turned on the Internet lately? Poppy checked in from her vacation in Fiji."

I knew the check-in was likely invented, but it was worth it just to see the flash of shock on Cash's face. He quickly recovered, but the damage was done. "What news outlet is reporting this?"

"Oh, it's not a news outlet. It's a gossip blog. Celebrity Burn." I brushed my hand down the front of my blouse. "The blogger, Rubee, was around here yesterday. You should definitely ask her about that."

Yes, sic Cash on Rubee. With any luck, I'd be within earshot. I took a sip of my coffee to keep from smiling.

"Those blogs are unreliable," Cash said, sounding unconvinced.

"Well, what do I know? It's a thought. Maybe she knows something, or maybe she doesn't. If I'm not under arrest, though, I'd like to have my breakfast."

"Yeah, okay. Have a good day, then."

"You too."

I continued up the steps and into the trailer, locking the door behind me. An absurd conversation with Detective Cassius DeLuca was not the way I wanted to begin my morning. I nearly shrieked when I saw the man lounging on my couch.

"Oh, hey, Wren. I figured I'd let myself in," Jax said casually as he set a stack of papers down across his chest. "Are you two finally done talking?"

Beneath my hand, I could feel my heart hammering in my chest as I struggled to catch my breath. "You just let yourself in? You scared me half to death."

"Sorry about that. I was hoping to surprise you in a good way."

I couldn't be angry with him when he smiled like that. "No, you did. It's okay."

He pointed to the plate in my hand. "Are those all for you?"

I handed them over without another word. He selected a coffee cake muffin. "You'll be happy to know that I'm back in Hodges's good graces."

"Oh yeah?" I ducked to the dressing area in the back of the trailer and selected my designer clothes for the day. "Why is that?"

"The ink is drying on my contract to play Ben in *The Rose Garden*."

"Jax." I peeked out at him from over the curtain. "That's wonderful! Really, it's the best news I've heard in a long time!" I ran over to the couch and flung my arms around him. "You're perfect for the role. I mean it."

He chuckled and gave me a warm kiss on the lips. "Of course you had something to do with it. I'm now known on the blogs as Wren Mallory's boyfriend, but hey

— I'll take it. They think you smell like roses, and I've become blameless by association."

I chuckled as I ducked back behind the curtain and selected a white tunic top and leggings. It wasn't my normal garb, but it looked comfortable, and I was craving comfort. "It's ridiculous, this fiction that's emerged about my life all because I date you and saved Poppy from drowning in a swimming pool. Those bloggers don't know a single thing about me."

"Don't question it, baby doll," he said easily. "Part of succeeding in life is knowing when to keep your mouth shut."

"Isn't that the truth."

I finished dressing and stepped around the curtain. I sat beside Jax, tucking my feet up and nuzzling my cheek against his shoulder. "You could've saved me out there, you know. With Cash."

"How would I have done that?" He broke off a generous piece of topping and dropped it into his mouth.

"I don't know," I admitted. "Kicked us off the steps, 'get-off-my-lawn' style? Better yet, you could've asked me to come in alone."

A slow smile spread across his lips. "Where's the fun of that? I was enjoying the drama of the scene. It's like something out of one of those cop shows."

I intertwined my fingers with his and groaned. "Did you hear him? He thinks Poppy is dead and that I killed her."

"I didn't say it was a *good* cop show." He set the muffin down on a napkin on an end table beside the couch and pulled the manuscript he'd been reading onto his lap. "You didn't kill Poppy. But I think you're close to killing with this screenplay. I mean that in the nicest way, you know."

The blood rushed to my feet in a rapid chill. He'd been reading my screenplay. "That — I didn't give that to you." I reached across and grabbed it out of his hands. "Jeezus. That's not cool, Jax. It's still a work in progress."

My fingers were trembling and my face was hot. I wasn't ready to share my screenplay yet, and he'd just let himself into the trailer and picked it up without permission. "Not cool," I repeated, softer this time.

Jax slung one arm across the back of the couch, his legs splayed, as he watched my discomfort. I expected him to laugh or tell me how misguided I was for feeling the way I did, but he didn't. He tilted his head to the side and said, "I didn't know what to expect when we made our deal. There are so many aspiring writers with a screenplay. But you're actually good."

I wrapped my hands around the screenplay and held it against my chest, poor armor for whatever critical assault he was preparing to launch in my direction. "I don't want to talk about this. Not with you."

"Why not?" He lifted his shoulders. "I'm as good a reader as anyone else, and I like to think I know something about the business."

"I've put a lot of work into this, okay?" My voice was pinched. "I'm not ready to put it out for discussion."

My face was steaming hot, and I'd gone from enjoying the easy rapport with Jax to wanting him to leave so I could bury my face in a pillow and cry. As if he could read my mind, he said, "There's no need to be so sensitive. I'm not going to attack you. I liked the story, and I thought the writing was fantastic."

Perhaps I was being a little sensitive. I released my breath slowly, cautiously. "Then what's wrong with it?"

"It's not you, that's what's wrong with it." He leaned forward until his elbows were on his knees. "There's a time traveling element, and that's cool, but then there's all of this background drama, this person seducing that one, this third character trying to trick this corporate guy into giving her a job."

"I'm trying to add layers." I hated that I sounded so wounded, but I needed to defend myself. "It's supposed to enhance the story."

"Yeah, but it ends up detracting from the heart of the story. The romance." He watched me from below his brows. "It's there, but it's like you don't want to face it. You second-guess it."

I chewed on my lower lip as I considered the question. He was right — the screenplay was a little bit...confused. "I've struggled with this," I confided. "I want to write something that's going to sell."

"Right. But what's here —" he drew a circle around my heart. "That's worth buying. Be honest."

"Honesty isn't my strong suit." I stuffed the screenplay into my bag and zipped it shut.

"You know, I don't understand that about you," Jax said. "You're lovely."

I laughed drily. "That's nice of you to say, but I don't see it that way. Everything I touch falls apart. My career, my relationships —" I paused as I thought about Jax. Was my luck about to change? I could only hope that I wouldn't screw that up the way I'd screwed up everything else. "Let's just say that sometimes it feels easier to be someone else. Someone who doesn't have the baggage I do."

"You rise to every challenge that confronts you. Why wouldn't honesty be your strong suit? What are you hiding from?"

I started to chew on my thumbnail, but stopped. Someone in makeup would have a fit if I messed up my polish. Instead, I folded my hands across my stomach. "I don't know," I said. At least it was true. "Look, I appreciate your belief in me and your comments on my screenplay. I don't want a therapy session, though."

"Fair enough." He stretched back out on the couch and clasped his hands behind his head. "I'm afraid of what I'd find if I opened your head and started tinkering."

"Oh really? Like instructions for how to make a mean macchiato?"

"More like fear. Hesitation." He snaked his arm across my waist to draw me onto his lap. "Complete denial about what's happening between us. Who could blame you, really?" He tucked my hair gently behind my ears. "I'm Hollywood's next big star, and you're the girl from the wrong side of the tracks, riding a shitty bicycle and obeying strict orders from a repressed police detective not to leave town."

I punched him lightly on the upper arm. "I can't ride that shitty bike anymore because you sold it for scrap."

"I actually sent it back to three decades ago. Where it belongs."

"That's theft. I'm going to press charges with Detective DeLuca, you know." I paused. "Just as soon as he considers me credible."

Jax chuckled softly. "Looks like I just got away with it."

I wanted to be angry with him for reading my screenplay without permission, except the more I thought about his criticism, the more I knew he was right. I was afraid. I'd spent my life afraid and hiding, and maybe it was time to try something else. Maybe I was overdue for a change.

CHAPTER EIGHTEEN

LOU HAD ONLY just finished applying my makeup when there was a knock at the trailer door. Brennan's assistant Cheryl burst in. "Wren? Hodges is looking for you." She pointed a clipboard at Jax. "You're on the invite list too."

Jax and I exchanged a glance. "Do we need to go now?" I said. "We're supposed to be filming —"

Cheryl arched one razor-thin eyebrow. "I'm sure Hodges will cover for you with Alex. But I don't want to keep him waiting, so *vamanos*."

Jax and I rose obediently and walked outside to the waiting golf cart. Cheryl darted down the steps after us and sat in the driver's seat. With a jerk, we were off. "Yeah, I have them," she said, pressing on an earpiece I hadn't noticed before. "We'll be there in two minutes."

We sped down the set, undeterred by workers and actors crossing the road. When she saw them, Cheryl simply waved them out of the way and continued. I suspected she even sped up. "What's this about?" I ventured.

"Sorry, I can't hear you."

"I said, what's this —"

She shot me a sidelong glare. "Not you. I'm on the phone." She pressed her finger to the earpiece. "Yeah, sorry about that. Can you repeat what you just said?"

It was as good an answer as any I would have gotten if she'd been giving her undivided attention, I suppose. I gripped the metal rail by my seat as we spun suddenly to the right and stopped at a blue door. Cheryl jumped out, still chattering away to herself.

"I guess we're here," I mumbled to Jax as I slid out of my seat. The drive may have been short, but it had been harrowing nonetheless.

Jax ambled out of the back, looking bored as ever. It occurred to me that I didn't know what he did with his days, aside from hanging out in my trailer and trying not to pick up strange women. He was checking his phone as we approached the blue door.

Cheryl opened the door and allowed us to walk past her. She was still talking. "Uh huh. I told them it was no good. If I come down there and see that it hasn't been fixed, it's not going to be pretty." She pointed down the hall. "This way."

We followed her around a few turns to a door marked "H. Brennan." Cheryl rapped on the door three times and waited. From the other side, we heard a muffled, "Come in," and entered.

This was a corner office, but the view — a glimpse at a small grassy plot and a duck pond with a fountain — wasn't much to look at. The windows on both sides of the room stretched almost floor to ceiling and they admitted a generous amount of sunlight, but as we entered, Hodges was pulling the blinds to half-shut. He was standing behind a large L-shaped desk on which were scattered various piles of papers and folders. One of the windowless walls was equipped with three file cabinets. The office was generally undecorated, drab, and not at all what I would have expected from someone as powerful as Brennan was. I assumed it was a remote office that he used while on set, and I might have asked him about it, but I saw by the stern pull of his mouth that this was no time for chitchat. He pointed to a table in the corner around which were four chairs and said, "Have a seat."

We were in the principal's office again, and my heart pattered about as I racked my brain, trying to recall anything I'd done that would've resulted in this meeting. Maybe I was a horrible actress, but I'd never pretended to be any good, had I? I tugged at the ends of my hair.

Brennan looked at Cheryl with a glower. "Where's Greta? I thought I told her —"

Cheryl looked out into the hallway. "I see her. She's coming now."

He waited, watching the door like an angry parent waiting for the child who'd missed curfew. Momentarily,

Greta shuffled inside in a bright pink sundress and silver sandals, her platinum hair stylishly pulled back in a chignon. "Sorry, am I late?" she asked with a smile. "Hodges. You're looking well." His mouth tightened, but Greta proceeded to the table with a little wave to us, trailing a cloud of citrusy perfume. "Morning, morning," she said.

"Morning," I replied.

"This isn't a reunion," Hodges bellowed. He pointed to Cheryl, who wordlessly left the room, closing the door behind her. "We've got a big problem."

Greta sighed and cocked her head, slinging one slender leg over the other. "Whatever it is, it can be fixed. If this is about Wren's union status, I've been working —"

"Stop talking, Greta. I had an interesting chat with Rubee this morning."

"Rubee's a lot of hot air," Greta said, with a sidelong glance at me.

"I'm not taking an opinion poll. She said —"

He broke off at the sound of a loud argument in the hallway. Seconds later, the door burst open. Beside me, Jax mumbled, "Oh shit."

Standing in the doorway was a tall, lean woman. It didn't take long for the panic to set in. *Poppy.*

"Hello, bitches," she said with a frosty smile. "Fun and games are over."

Hodges leaned against his desk, his arms folded tightly across his chest. Greta, Jax, and I were seated at the conference table. All eyes were on Poppy, who was holding court in the center of the room.

She may have arrived like a hurricane, but she did look better than she had when I'd seen her two weeks ago. Less intoxicated, at least. She stood poised like a sculpture and took a long sip from a huge plastic water bottle. Then she made a show of replacing the cap. It was kind of like watching a geyser bubble: the question wasn't whether it would erupt in a violent spasm of dangerously hot water, but when.

She looked at Hodges with a twisted smirk on her lips. "Aren't you going to say you're happy to see me?"

His frown deepened and his face darkened. "As far as I'm concerned, you're trespassing on this set."

"Then call security." She walked behind his desk and poised her finger above a button on his phone. "Do you want me to call?" When he didn't respond, she chuckled softly and said, "I didn't think so." She peered out between the blinds. "This view sucks."

"If you have something to say, then say it," Hodges said. "Otherwise, get the hell out of my office."

"Whatever." Poppy returned to the center of the room, this time to seat herself on a short wooden filing cabinet. "I've been at the spa. I've also been sober for almost two weeks now. Thanks for noticing how fantastic I look," she said wryly.

"One day at a time," Hodges said. "Though usually rehab programs are longer than fourteen days."

"Yes. That's true." Her blonde hair was pulled back in a side braid, and she toyed at the ends as she thought. "They have strict rules at these places, too. No Internet. No contact with the outside world. I do hate rules. I made it until last night without checking the Internet, but then I demanded my cell phone. My mistake, because then I learned about *this*." She gestured to the rest of us in the room. "This betrayal."

Hodges rolled his eyes and rounded his desk. "Always with the melodrama. Unfortunately for you, a certain blogger tipped me off and told me she'd spoken with you and you were on your way, so your appearance isn't much of a surprise. You breached your contract by failing to appear on the set. I don't give a goddamn what you think about me hiring a replacement."

"No, I wouldn't think so," she said. "But it's the *type* of replacement you hired." Poppy's tongue licked into the corner of her mouth and she grinned a wicked, mean smile. "She's not even an actress. She's a barista at a local dive. A nobody."

The words sliced right through me. I'd had enough. I jumped to my feet and shouted, "You. Shut up."

The outburst wiped that evil smile right off her face. She was speechless, which gave me enough time to continue. "You. Do you even know what I've risked for you? I kept your damn secret. No one even knew you were in rehab."

"I knew," Jax muttered quietly.

"Okay, fine," I said. "Jax knew. But the point is you asked me to keep a secret and I did. And how dare you come in here and say that I'm a nobody. I'm a bigger person than you'll ever be."

A heavy silence loomed. I could tell that Poppy hadn't expected me to actually stand up to her. Most people probably didn't. Rather than respond to me, she turned her attention to Hodges. "What happens now, Hodges?"

"We've already started filming," he said casually, leaning back in his chair. "If I were you, I'd leave the set right now. You're lucky I haven't decided to sue you, but I could always change my mind."

Poppy stared at a spot on the carpet, deflated. I wondered what she had expected when she'd come storming in here — a hug? Tears of happiness? Then I realized that this was everything that she'd feared: that she'd vanish, and life would continue without her. That she'd barely be missed at all.

Jax sighed and shook his head. "Too bad, Poppy. You've been replaced." I felt him set a hand protectively against my back. "The worst part is that Wren is a better actress than you."

I swear, a shadow crossed her face. I actually witnessed the rage setting in. "Thanks, Jax," she said in an icy voice. "Tell me, have you told Wren here about our history?"

"Your..." My mouth went completely dry. I looked at Jax, but he wasn't looking at me. He was staring at Poppy, slack-jawed. My heart sank. "You and Poppy?" I squeaked.

Poppy laughed. "No, we were never an item. Trust me, I wasn't interested." She stepped closer, closing in on us. "Jax, don't you remember that party we met at? It was right after Griff had been discovered, as they say, and you were telling him that it was high time he settle on...how did you put it? A better piece of real estate." She smiled brightly. "Am I remembering correctly?"

Greta cleared her throat and stood. "Hey, Wren, let's get out and let them talk —"

"This concerns her," Poppy snapped. "In every way. Because you know what, honey? Jax Cosgrove is the one who told Griff that he needed to dump his homely girlfriend and date someone with actual star potential."

I don't know if Poppy continued talking after that. I couldn't hear her above the pounding in my ears. I was still staring at Jax, watching for his reaction. The fact that he wouldn't look at me told me everything. "Oh my god."

I stumbled to my feet, took a second to find my balance, and headed numbly out the door. By the time I reached the middle of the hallway, I heard Jax say, "Wait!" But I kept walking.

The tears spilled as I headed down the hallway, awash with self-pity. This was disaster, and it was all of my making. *Fool.* Plus, my sandals were too small and my feet were nearly blistering already. I pushed open the door to the back lot and blinked into the daylight. The sun was peeking through the clouds, which should have made me feel optimistic somehow. It didn't.

I wiped off my tears, leaving a trail of foundation, mascara, and eyeliner on my fingers, which I then wiped on my white tunic. If I was going to be a hot mess, then I may as well embrace it. Cheryl had left the golf cart parked in the lot, the key in the ignition.

"Wren!" Jax ran to the front of the golf cart and set his hands on the hood. "Wait. Please."

"You should move. No one would blame me if I ran you over right now." I hated that he was seeing how much he hurt me, because then he'd know how much I cared. "Go away, Jax."

"It was a stupid thing for me to have said to Griff."

"So it's true?" There went any last shred of hope. "You told him to break up with me?"

"It wasn't personal, I swear. I didn't even know you. I'd never even seen you!"

"But all this time." A faucet turned on and the tears flowed freely now. "We've been together for all this time, and you never said a word." I shook my head. "Don't you get it? I thought Griff was a troll, but at least he was big enough not to tell me what a liar my current boyfriend is."

I covered my eyes with my fingers, feeling the grime of makeup smudging. Not that I cared anymore. I was finished caring, when all it got me was a fist twisting my heart in place.

"I'm sorry. I don't know what else to say." Jax stood, allowing his arms to hang limply at his side. "I should've told you. I didn't want you to hate me."

My hands were white-knuckled on the steering wheel. "Why should I believe anything you say when you only look out for yourself?" I took a shaking breath and looked him in the eye. "To think I actually allowed myself to care about you. Please move out of my way. Now."

I wanted him to get on his knees and beg me for forgiveness, or take me into his arms and swear that he wasn't just another vain, self-absorbed actor. Instead, he stepped away from the cart to allow me passage. I stepped on the pedal and sped away, trying to ignore the painful ache in my chest.

CHAPTER NINETEEN

I CAUGHT A ride back to town with Emily, who had been just packing up to leave the studio. Jessie was out in the parking lot, checking her watch, when we pulled in. She had opened the back doors before the engine was off. "Em, we've got to hurry. The place has been hopping this morning and Zack called out sick." I heard the sound of empty trays being removed. "We're not going to get lunch there in time."

I slid out of the van and shut the door behind me. "Hey, Jess."

Her head appeared from behind the vehicle, surprise evident in her wide eyes. "Wren? What's going on?"

"I wanted to come back here." My footsteps on the gravel sounded louder than usual.

Jessie frowned with concern. "Why, are you feeling sick? You look pale." She reached out to clasp a palm on my forehead. "You feel a little warm."

"I'm fine." I brought her hand down with mine. "Really," I added when her lips tightened in disbelief.

"Go in and sit down. Have something to drink. Have you had lunch yet?"

I loaded my arms with trays and platters. "I'm going to help you. I told you, I'm fine. I just want to work here this afternoon."

Jessie clearly wasn't buying it, but we had too much to do to indulge in follow-up conversation. After a few trips between the van and the kitchen, Jessie, Emily, and I managed to load the lunch order in record time. As Emily pulled out of the lot, Jessie wrapped an arm around my shoulders and said, "Now. You want to tell me what's going on?"

Yes, I did, but this was a discussion that would take a while. "I'm sure the bakery is busy. How about if we talk later?"

I avoided eye contact, knowing the suggestion would raise immediate suspicion. When it came to bakery staff, Emily was the hero. She brewed coffee, waited tables, and cheerfully prepared sandwiches. I, on the other hand, had refused to do most of those things, citing my incompetence as an excuse.

"You want to cover for Emily?" Jessie's eyes narrowed. "Did you bump your head or something?"

"No," I said, filing the suggestion away for a future screenplay. I stopped and spun to face her. "I just think it's time that I stop acting like a damn special snowflake. What has my contribution been to this business? I foam lattes and brew coffee, and somehow convince my mom that she should spend her time sprucing up the space. And for some reason Dad pays me hourly." I paused and remembered the little plastic jar on the counter. "Plus tips."

"Wren, where's this coming from?" Jessie put her hands on my upper arms and gave a light squeeze. "Honey, you're not a charity case, and you're not acting like a special snowflake."

"Yes, I am. Don't look at me like that," I said with a sigh. "Like I'm all dramatic or something."

"You *are* dramatic. Your whole life is like something out of some made-for-television movie."

Some part of that statement reverberated in a satisfying way. "It's true," I said. "But I'm not trying to be dramatic right now. I'm trying to do the right thing. The honest thing."

My cousin tilted her head to the side, still not entirely convinced. "Something's up, but okay. Let's go back to work."

"Thanks, Jess."

As we walked side by side, I ached to tell her everything. Jessie was the sister I'd never had, the friend who'd always shared my secrets. But I knew that the moment I told her about Jax, I'd only be unloading my burden onto her shoulders. I owed it to her to at least wait until the bakery was closed for the day.

"Don't think I'm letting you off the hook," she teased as we tied our aprons in the kitchen. "The truth comes out eventually."

She laughed, and a pain spread in my chest. Still, I forced a smile and walked into the bakery.

I survived my afternoon as Emily's replacement. More than survived. I waited and bussed tables, brewed coffee, and prepared some sandwiches. True, I brought the wrong lunch order to table seven, but that was remedied with a quick and sincere apology and a few chocolate chunk cookies on the house. When three o'clock rolled around, I was happy to lock the door and turn the sign to "closed" — that is, until I remembered what had to come next.

"Jessie?" Dad's voice called from the kitchen. "Did you talk to Brown's Farm about that order of blueberries?"

Jessie was zeroing out the till. She called back over her shoulder, "He said he's going to bring them tomorrow."

Dad came into the doorway and rested one elbow high on the doorjamb. "So what do we make tonight if we don't have blueberries?"

"We have currants. I thought we could use those. And the strawberries are still good."

Dad's face looked drawn as he wiped his hands on his apron, and my heart tugged with concern. Here I thought

I'd been doing the right thing, the heroic thing, by cutting a deal with Hodges Brennan for that catering contract, but these long hours were clearly taking a toll on him. His face looked ashen, his hair disheveled. "Dad? Why don't you head home for a while?"

He looked at me as though he wasn't registering the words, then turned and walked back into the kitchen. I pulled up beside Jessie as she counted money. "What's going on with Dad? Is he all right?"

"He's tired. We're all tired." She suppressed a yawn. "Excuse me."

Jessie held up a finger and I waited while she finished her count, stuffed a handful of bills into an envelope, and shut the drawer. "He hasn't had a day off in months. I'm trying to convince him to take a few days after next week, when we're done with that catering job." She tucked a loose strand of hair behind her ear. "The contract has been great, but it hasn't been easy. I don't need to tell you that, though."

She headed into the kitchen, so I cleaned up the coffee area, wiped down the counters, and washed the pitchers in the sink. The task took me longer than usual, not only because I was procrastinating, but because I wanted to do a good job. I needed to at least do that much. Finally, there were no more surfaces to be scrubbed or disinfected. I wrung out the rag and threw it in a bucket to be washed. Then I walked to the kitchen.

"Hey, you guys?" I set the bucket on the floor. "Do you think we could have a few minutes to talk?"

Dad was sifting flour into a mixing bowl. "Sure, honey. What's going on?"

I looked over at Jessie, who was washing dishes in the sink. "Jess? Can you come here for a few minutes?"

"Give me a sec," she said over her shoulder. "I'm almost finished."

I pulled up a stool and took a seat. My fingertips were like ice, and I brought them into my lap in a futile effort to warm them. I tried to rehearse my speech. I had to let them know that it was over between me and Jax, and that it had never been real in the first place. I'd tell the truth, simply and openly, that's all.

As I waited for Jessie to finish, I heard a voice call out, "Hello? Okay to come in?" Seconds later, Mom opened the door, carrying two large shopping bags. "I have some window treatments," she said. "And Jess, I have someone coming tomorrow morning to remove that wood paneling in the apartment upstairs. Hopefully it's easy come, easy go."

"Do I need to stay somewhere else?"

"No, he should be done tomorrow." Mom pulled some fabric out of the bag and set it on the counter. "Hey, sweetheart," she said to me.

"Hey, Mom."

"Don't I get a hello?" Dad asked, feigning injury.

The side of Mom's mouth quirked upward. "Hello."

"Hi, Lil." He smiled.

"Well, if you don't mind, I'm going to get down to work," Mom said as she swept one of the bags into her arms. "I have a client meeting at five, but I think I can make it on time if I hurry."

She swept into the bakery, and dad looked up from his mixing to watch her. I was still ruminating on that odd fact moments later when Emily came in, her eyes wide. Jessie noticed immediately. "Emily? Is everything okay?"

That was when I observed her trembling fingers. Still, she had the presence of mind to hang the van keys on the key rack before fumbling for a stool. "I — I don't know what happened." Her chin trembled and she burst into tears. "They told me not to come back."

"What?" I rose from my stool and hurried to her side. "Who told you that? What did they say?"

She was sobbing, her lips blubbering as she struggled to catch her breath. "I — don't know her name. She said she was an assistant or something. She told me that they'd decided to go with a different caterer, beginning tomorrow." I handed Emily a tissue and she swept it under her eyes and nose.

"An assistant?" I asked. "Was it an executive assistant? Maybe named Cheryl?"

"Probably. Yes. I don't know." She inhaled shakily. "I'm so sorry. I don't know what I did wrong."

"Shh," Jessie assured her as she came over to Emily's side. "You didn't do anything wrong. I promise." She looked at Dad. "I don't understand. Do you have any idea what this is about?"

"No." Dad's hands were pulled into fists, his jaw tightly clenched. "But this isn't the end of it. They think they're dealing with some small bakery in a hick town? I'll sue them for breach of contract before they know what's hit them." He flung his apron onto the counter. "They don't know who they're messing with."

"Dad." I didn't like how red his face was getting. "Dad. Please, calm down."

"Let me handle this, Wren." He headed to the back of the kitchen, to a little alcove where he kept a desk, a computer, and some files. "I'm going to get that contract and call them right now. Find out what happened."

I took a breath. "I can tell you what happened."

I felt Jessie and Emily's gaze on me, but Dad didn't hear. He came back into view moments later, gripping the contract in his hands. "Here it is. Now, see? In section ten —"

"Dad. *Dad*," I repeated, this time placing a hand on his. "I know what's going on. I can explain it."

"Wren, whatever you did is no excuse —"

"Uncle Hank," Jessie said, eyeing me steadily. "Let her explain."

He looked up from the contract, and Emily and Jessie waited. So I took a deep breath, and I told them everything.

Silence. That was the response. I'd expected shouting, or at least some elevated voices, but by the time I reached the end of my sad tale, all I heard was silence. "So, that's it. Jax and I made a deal, but we were a complete lie, and today I walked off the set. So now you know everything," I said, giving the cue that it was all right to speak.

The silence stretched on for what felt like a hundred violent heartbeats. I chewed on my bottom lip as I waited, passing my gaze from Emily's open mouth and wide eyes to Jessie's troubling refusal to make eye contact to Dad's complexion, which was a shade of light eggplant. Mom had joined us a few minutes into the tale, and she was standing to the side, leaning back against the sink and studying me, her face lined with thoughts I couldn't read.

I cleared my throat. "I'm sorry. I didn't mean — I got in over my head."

"Honey."

Dad stepped forward, and the next thing I knew, my face was buried in his shoulder. "You have nothing to apologize for."

That started the tears again. "We needed this catering contract, and I blew it."

"No! Have you seen the crowds?" I felt Jessie's hand on my back. "Whatever happened with Jax, you've saved this bakery. Hedda's is a destination now."

"Honey," Mom said gently, "you've turned this entire business around. Who cares who you're fake dating? That's between you and Jax. Will you still appear in the movie?"

The sound of his name hurt. I slumped onto a stool. "No. I didn't finish filming my scenes, and now Poppy's back so I guess she'll get the role. They'll reshoot the scenes I was in."

"I have to ask: was this about Griff?" Mom's brow furrowed. "Deep down, is that what this was all about?"

"Uh, no, Mom. It wasn't about Griff. It was about seizing an opportunity and making the most of it." I swallowed. "You know? I wanted to succeed at something for a change. I thought if I could get my screenplay in front of Hodges Brennan, maybe I'd get a shot at the career I've always wanted. I thought I could help the bakery." I looked at Dad. "Do we have to sell?"

He smiled and patted my hair fondly. "No, honey. Assuming this business keeps up, we're in the clear. You're a hero."

I smiled weakly for the first time in hours. I'd saved Hedda's, and that was something.

Food prep for the next day wasn't nearly what it had been when we were catering the set, so when we left at seven, the night felt young. "I don't even know what I'm going to do with myself," I said to Jessie as I shut the door behind us. "I'll probably stay up until midnight for the hell of it."

When I turned the lock, I thought about walking back to my apartment alone, turning on the lights, preparing a meal for one, and then climbing into the bed that Jax and I had just shared. I could have buried myself in self-pity just then. Jessie shifted quietly beside me. "Do you want to come up for dinner?"

"Nah, I'm beat. Maybe another time." I felt more nauseous than hungry, anyway. I made a feeble attempt at a grin. "Have a good night."

Jessie tilted her head to one side. "You may have fooled some people, but you didn't fool me. Everything that was happening between you and Jax was real, wasn't it?"

"Yeah, well." I cleared the lump in my throat. "Maybe for one of us."

She reached out and gently clasped my fingers. "Do you want to talk about it?"

There were lots of reasons not to. My pride, for one. I'd gone and allowed Griff to stomp on my heart, and then I'd gone and allowed Jax to do the same thing. "What is it with me and actors, Jess?" I whispered. "I should be in psychotherapy."

"You definitely should, but I don't think for this." She smiled and smoothed a hand down my shoulder. "Jax Cosgrove is one of the hottest guys around. Who wouldn't hear angels when he entered the room? Have you noticed how Emily can't even look him in the eyes? He's intimidatingly gorgeous."

"No." I shook my head. "He's not intimidating. At all. He's got this bad-boy thing, but it's an act. He's thoughtful and kind of sweet, and —" I trailed off when I saw the knowing look on Jessie's face. "It doesn't matter. It's over, and I'm going to go date someone stable and boring." The image of Cash DeLuca flitted across my mind. I shuddered. "Not *too* boring. Nice boring."

Jessie rolled her eyes heavenward and said, "Oh, sure. Date someone stable and boring and let me know how that goes. You, my friend, crave the drama. Come on."

She pulled at my hand and took a step toward the stairs to her apartment. "I ordered takeout last night and it will feed both of us *and* your bad feelings. Besides, Prince Travis misses you."

The steps I took behind her didn't feel reluctant. More like grateful. "Okay. But just so you know, I'm only coming up to help you eat your leftovers, not because I'm upset or anything."

"No, of course," she said over her shoulder. "But just so *you* know, I'm going to pressure you to spend the night on my extremely comfortable couch, and I'm planning to open a bottle of wine to make it harder for you to say no. So what's it going to be, red or white?"

"White," I quickly replied.

Jessie laughed quietly. "I thought so. I have some chilling as we speak."

CHAPTER TWENTY

Iᴛ's ɴᴏᴛ ʟɪᴋᴇ I'd gone running to the media about my broken heart, but somehow, people knew.

By mid-morning, the bakery was filled with cellophane-wrapped flowers and cards expressing good wishes. "Another bouquet," Emily announced as she brought a bunch of white sweetheart roses into the kitchen. "I don't know where we're going to put all of them."

I didn't either. I'd been nearly teary-eyed at the thoughtfulness of the first few bunches of flowers, and I put them in Mason jars and decorated the tables with them. I may have had a mild hangover from my night at Jessie's, but it wasn't enough to distract me from the many simple, lovely gestures from strangers expressing their sadness that the local coffee girl's brush with celebrity had ended.

I lifted the bouquet from Emily's arms. "I'll cut the stems. I think we can add these to the Mason jars."

When I was finished, I stepped back to admire the arrangements. The flowers looked so beautiful, and they filled the space with rainbow hues of warm wishes from strangers.

"It's a family bakery," I heard one patron whisper to another as they waited in line at the counter. "An old-fashioned place, where everyone knows you."

"Oh," her companion responded. "I love places like this. It feels like home."

I smiled. Dad and Jessie would be so pleased.

We were talking about extending bakery hours, at least for the summer. With the crowds the way they were, it didn't feel like a choice. As it was, we were staying open well past closing time on most nights. We'd called in reinforcements, past employees who were home from college and willing to help out to get us through the crunch. For the most part, they were waiting tables and running orders. Jessie was baking in the back, Emily was at the register, and I was preparing coffees. Business as usual.

"Skinny mocha!" Emily called out beside me.

"Coming up."

Mom came in after lunch and pitched in wherever needed. She washed dishes and cleared tables, and she didn't even mind it. Actually, she looked happier than I could ever remember seeing her. "How are you holding up, sweetheart?" she asked me as she refilled the pastry display with white chocolate cherry scones.

"I'm fine," I said. "Did you talk to Dad? He seemed a little overwhelmed this morning. He may need help in back."

"You know your father. He insists he can handle it. If I try to help him, it's just a burden in the hand." She paused to adjust her blue gloves. "You're probably wondering what's going on between us."

I glanced across the counter to see whether anyone was listening in, but fortunately there was a break in the lunch crowd, and the line had dwindled. Still, I lowered my voice. "I think I know."

"Can I tell you anyway?" She let her hands drop to her side and proceeded without waiting for permission. "I don't know what it is, but when I saw him a few weeks ago, it was like all of these feelings came back. He felt it, too. This sense that we'd let too much life get by us while we were caught up harboring old resentment."

I leaned against the counter, absently turning a silver milk pitcher in my hands. "I like seeing you two together again."

"Me too." She brightened, and I wondered if she'd actually feared that I would disapprove. "In some ways it feels like coming home again."

"And I'm sure I've given you a lot of things to discuss these days," I noted wryly. "I like to think I've helped to break the ice."

The spot between her brows creased. "We couldn't be more proud of you, Wren. You're figuring your life out and pursuing your dreams with everything you have. Look at this crowd. You did this."

I followed the sweep of her hand as she gestured to the bakery around us. "I love this place. I grew up here."

She pulled my head forward to kiss me on the cheek. "It's growing on me too. Hey!" She snaked an arm around my waist. "I was thinking we should talk about branching out a bit. With catering. I've picked up quite a few recipes over the years, and I could practically teach a class in French cuisine."

"You want to start a side business, Mom?" I grinned. "You'll need to talk to Jessie. She's in charge of the catering, and I'm sure she'd be thrilled to have some help."

That night, we closed at seven. Bone weary and yawning, I mustered the effort to avoid sitting down with Jessie and opening another bottle of wine. Sooner or later, I was going to have to return to my apartment alone.

It was home, I reminded myself. Even behind Crabby Andy's, even smelling like a fish fry, this apartment was my home. I should have been happy to near it, but every step closer filled me with dread, because even if this was *my* home, Jax had left his impression. I thought of him as I mounted the stairs and as I stepped into the kitchen. I thought of him on the way to the bedroom, and I fought the memories as I changed the bedsheets. I should have vacuumed and scrubbed. I should have spent the night, as tired as I was, removing all microscopic traces of him. But it was futile.

I took a hot shower and climbed into bed. The last thing I did before turning out the lights was check my cell phone for missed calls. Nothing from Jax. I pretended it didn't hurt.

Four days after storming off the set, I was too busy preparing a Caffè Americano to notice the tall, dark figure crossing the street. I only looked up when I heard the screams outside. It was Jax. He graciously stopped to sign a few autographs and pose for a couple pictures before continuing inside. The shrieks of recognition followed him, but to my amazement, the room went silent as he entered and crossed over to the counter where I was working. My heart was beating so hard that I had to set down the cup I was washing.

He took deliberate care removing his aviator glasses, keeping his dark eyes on me the entire time, a hesitant smile playing on his lips. "Hello, Wren," he said.

I turned to face him, keeping my chin raised. "Hello, Jax," I said, softly. "It's nice to see you."

Behind me, I was vaguely aware of Emily, breathless and still. All around us, eyes were watching. I'd be lying if I said it wasn't exhilarating.

Jax glanced around the bakery as if the crowd was nothing unusual, and yet patrons had set down their forks and cups, turned their heads and craned their necks and stilled their conversations, all to watch us. "Is there somewhere we can go to talk?"

I gestured casually to the room. "I'm a little busy right now. Can we talk later?"

He followed my gesture and inched closer, lowering his voice to a stage whisper. "I miss you."

Around me, the mostly-female audience sighed appreciatively. A few pressed their hands against their hearts. "Jax." I looked down and away. "You know it's for the best."

You could've heard a crumb drop. There was a collective intake of breath as he shifted his weight from one foot to the other. Then he leaned forward and gently set his hands on my cheeks, gazing into my eyes. I stifled a nervous laugh, but then I saw something, a flicker in his gaze, that stilled me. "I'm sorry a hundred times over. I'm an idiot," he said softly. "And since you left, I'm an idiot without a purpose, which is the worst kind."

Somehow, everything fell away. There we were, just the two of us. "I guess I'm sorry for telling Rubee that you wax your, uh..." I gestured helplessly and felt my face burn. "Your man region."

"That was you?" He rubbed at his forehead but then shook his head. "That doesn't matter. It's the least of what anyone has said about me. Listen, I told Alex Sherapovna all about your screenplay. Don't look shocked, it was part of the arrangement. He's very interested, and he's going to stop in before he leaves.

Probably sometime next week." He paused. "I told him I wanted to play Jude."

The romantic lead in my screenplay? "You do? Seriously?"

"Seriously. It's a great role." He grabbed my hands and pressed them together in his. "I can't stop thinking about you. Please, Wren, can't we go somewhere to talk?"

I looked over my shoulder and saw Jessie, wide-eyed, mouth the word, "GO!" and shoo me with one hand.

"Yeah," I said. "This way."

I led him into the kitchen. Dad looked up in confusion but didn't have time to get out more than "Hello!" before we'd passed through the doorway and into the back parking lot. My nerves were on fire, my heart sputtering around in my chest, but I tried to look indifferent as I spun around and said, "So? Is this private enough?"

He set his hands on my shoulders. "Close your eyes. Just trust me," he added as I opened my mouth to argue.

I released a heavy sigh but shut my eyes. He led me a few steps and turned me around. "All right. Open them."

There, below the staircase behind Hedda's, was a beautiful new bicycle. Purple, just like my old one, but this one was definitely brand new. On the seat was a giant white silk bow. "Oh, Jax." I clapped my hands over my mouth. "Is this for me?"

"It's only fair, considering I made you surrender your last one." He watched me as I ran my hands over the rim. "Do you like it? I tried to pick out something that you'd like. You seem to like purple, and bows. Girly stuff." He touched the handlebars absentmindedly. "They don't make bikes with tassels for adults. I checked. If you want them, I can have it special ordered. If you don't like the bike, I'll take it back. You should get whatever you want. I want you to be happy with it. Though I don't know what you're going to do when winter comes. You're going to need a car —"

I jumped into his arms and kissed him. I threw my arms around his broad shoulders, pulling him closer, wanting to prove to myself that he was really here, that *we* were finally real. When he broke off the kiss, we were both breathless. He rested his forehead against mine. "So you like the bike?"

"I love it. Thank you."

"I love *you*," he said. "I love you truly, with everything I am, for everything you are. You're sweet, and sensitive, and insecure about everything. But I love you for it, and I should have told you sooner."

Something caught in my throat. "I love you too. You're kind of arrogant." I paused as he chuckled. "But you're also thoughtful and kind. I have to say, when you fed me that line about being misunderstood, I didn't believe it, but now I can see. All those women, though —
"

"Like I said, an exaggeration," he whispered. "And in any case, that's over. There's only one woman for me." He softly kissed the back of my hand. "If you'll have me."

I rested my ear against his chest and listened to his heart. "I can't imagine what I'd do without you," I whispered. "Can I ask for one more thing?"

"What's that?"

I pulled back to look him in the eye. "Will you take me out for ice cream tonight?"

He chuckled and lifted me into his arms. "I'll buy you the world."

"Just the ice cream would be fine," I smiled. "And maybe dinner. Like, a real date."

He set me back down and cradled my chin in his hands. "Done and done."

EPILOGUE

WE MAY HAVE been in love, but we had some things to think about. Jax sold his house in LA, and we bought a vineyard with a farmhouse in Great Barrington, overlooking the ocean. We built a tasting room on the edge of the property, which Mom decorated, of course. We sell our wine and pair it with Jessie's chocolates.

Emily runs the operation while we're away, and we've been traveling a lot. Jax's star is very bright in Hollywood, and he had the luxury of having his choice of roles after breaking hearts in *The Rose Garden*. He still claims his favorite role was in my screenplay, which I titled *Love over Time*. I suspect he says that because he helped me develop the story so well. And truth be told, the part of Jude was made for him.

As for me, well...I'm not acting, though I did make my film debut in *The Office of Wayward Problems*, after all. Hodges had refused to recast Poppy and had instead reimagined my part based on the scenes I'd filmed. The movie did well at the box office, but I figure it's best to quit while I'm ahead. I'm happy writing my screenplays and staying out of the spotlight. Not because it's safe, but because it's where I like to be.

Griff and I have been friendly, if not exactly friends. Last I knew, he and Poppy were history and he was taking a break from Hollywood to spend time in India, meditating and finding himself. The tabloids reported that Poppy had successfully completed rehab and was developing her own line of makeup. I saw her one night as I was lying in bed flipping through the channels.

"Is that who I think it is?" Jax entered the room and stood still, staring at the television.

Poppy was smoothing cream into the area around her eyes and saying, "This takes care of the crow's feet. It's filled with microbeads that plump the area up —"

I sighed. "I feel like we should invite her to the wedding."

He began to undress. "I don't know about that."

"Consider this, though: if she and Griff hadn't dated, I never would have started dating you."

"Fair enough."

I rolled onto my side and smiled at him, at his sexy, confident grin and the muscles he was revealing one button at a time. "So we're getting married, then?"

He shrugged. "I always expected we would."

"Me too." I paused. "This isn't the proposal, is it?"

"Trust me, honey. When I propose, you'll know it." He peeled off his shirt and tossed it aside. "Promise me you'll never buy anything with microbeads for your crow's feet. At least, promise you won't do anything like that for me." He reached over and gently pried the remote control from my hands.

"You can be reasonably assured of that."

He clicked the television off and tossed the remote behind him. Then he set one knee on the bed and brought his lips hovering over mine. "Good, because I like you just the way you are."

He kissed me soundly on the lips and turned off the light. I could hardly argue with that.

* * * * *

A Note from the Author

THANK YOU FOR taking the time to read THE COFFEE GIRL! If you are so inclined, an honest review at the site of your choice would be appreciated.

If you want to know when my next book is out, please visit my website at nataliecharlesromance.com and sign up for my newsletter.

About the Author

NATALIE CHARLES HAS worked as an attorney, a playground supervisor, and a makeup sales clerk, but not in that order. The happy sufferer of a lifelong addiction to mystery novels, Natalie has, sadly, never out-sleuthed a detective. She is a RT Reviewer's Choice Award winner and a bestselling author of romantic suspense. She lives in Connecticut with her hero husband and two bookish children.

Natalie loves connecting with readers! You can find her on Facebook, facebook.com/writernataliecharles or Twitter @tallie_charles, or you can contact her through her website, nataliecharlesromance.com; or email at writernataliecharles@gmail.com.